C000216113

MISTLETOE MALARKEY

A SHAYLA MURPHY MYSTERY

STELLA BIXBY

This novel is a work of fiction. Names, characters, places, and incidents are either a product of the author's imagination or are used fictitiously. Any resemblance to actual persons, living or dead, businesses, events, or locales is entirely coincidental.

Copyright © 2021 by Crystal S. Ferry

All rights reserved.

No part of this book may be reproduced or transmitted in any form or by any means, electronic or mechanical, including photocopying, recording, or by any information storage and retrieval system presently available or yet to be invented without permission in writing from the publisher, except for the use of brief quotations in a book review.

❀ Created with Vellum

For the Brooklyn Library Book Club

F lying made me nervous.

Flying with the man of my dreams, who I suspected had an engagement ring in his pocket, gave me anxiety.

Flying to a new country for my favorite holiday to meet his entire family made me feel like I might have a full-blown panic attack.

Thankfully, Seamus held my hand and looked at me with his charming Irish stare that said—*Me eyes are only for you, Shayla.*

As the flight took off, his coffee tipped, spilling the entire contents of steaming liquid into his lap.

Not a single passenger batted an eye when he threw curses around like candy at a Fourth of July parade.

That was the Irish for you.

"Do you need to go to the bathroom and sort out your pants?" I asked Seamus, trying to help him mop it up with the teeny cocktail napkins.

"Only if yeh come and help me," he said in the Irish

brogue I was so in love with. Heck, I was in love with every-thing about him.

And he'd convinced me he loved everything about me.

It had been practically love at first sight.

Though I'd been about thirty pounds overweight, so I wasn't quite certain how it had been love at first sight for him—the gorgeous older foreign guy. But I'd since dropped the weight and was in the best shape of my life.

When I didn't respond to his suggestion, he shrugged. "I'll take care of it at the airport."

"I'm really excited to meet your family," I said.

"Yeh've told me about a thousand times." He laughed. "Now stop worryin' they're gonna love ya."

I stopped picking at my cuticles.

"And even if they don't," he said, "at least you get away from work for a while."

Just the thought of work made me cringe. "That is a plus." I was a police officer for the Prairie City Police Department. Just like my mom had been.

She was a PCPD legend. Everyone knew her name.

And, because of that, they knew mine.

When I'd started, everyone expected me to be just like her. Tough. Callous. Doesn't take no for an answer.

Too bad I was practically the opposite. Much to their disappointment.

Which meant I became a glorified coffee runner.

I tipped my head back on my seat. That would change. Eventually, they would appreciate the qualities I brought to the table. Even if they weren't the same as my mother's.

Seamus pushed a strand of my blonde hair behind my ear. I'd curled it like I did every day, but it had taken me twice as long. We'd almost missed our flight because I was so worried about how I looked.

"Don't think about work," he said. "I'm sorry I brought it up."

I turned and smiled at him.

He leaned over and kissed me softly on the lips. "You're beautiful."

"Thank you," I said. "I love you."

"And I adore you."

When the flight landed, we were almost the last ones off the airplane.

Seamus darted into the bathroom to clean up the coffee, leaving me to collect our luggage from the carousels.

Though the sun was peeking up over the horizon, my brain told me to go to bed immediately. I thought I'd be able to sleep on the airplane, but that proved to be unrealistic, given my state of worry.

I waited for our luggage to come around on the conveyor belt with several other people from our flight. I reached for Seamus' bag and pulled it off, almost running directly into a man who wasn't paying attention to what was going on around him.

Most of the people around the conveyor belt weren't paying attention to the circling luggage. All their heads pointed to the entrance, where it seemed someone very important had just arrived.

A glamorous woman stood by the doorway with gigantic sunglasses, stick-straight orange hair, and a figure to die for. She wore black platform sandals beneath hot pink bell-bottomed pants and a white off-the-shoulder top with tiered bell sleeves.

Several people next to me pulled out their phones to take photos of her as she posed for the paparazzi. They called out her name—which sounded like Eva only with an F in place of the V. Seamus had quizzed me about the spellings and pronunciations of Irish names several weeks before, and this was one of them. I highly suspected her name wasn't Eva with an F, but Aoife with an A at the beginning and a whole slew of other letters that didn't add up to the pronunciation in American terms.

Aoife lived up to the meaning of her name as well. She was the embodiment of beauty and radiance.

I glanced down at my trendy ripped jeans and oversized sweater and felt more like a slouch than a trendsetter.

"I heard her cousin is back in town," a woman next to me said.

It took me a moment to realize she was talking to me.

"Right," I said. "Her cousin."

"'Tis about time, if you ask me." She spoke in an Irish accent so thick I had to concentrate extra hard on what she was saying to understand her.

"Why's that?"

"He's been skirtin' his responsibilities, don't ya know," she said. "Needs to deal with the family business, and if he doesn't move quickly, he won't be the prime eligible bachelor in Ireland for long."

"Who is she?" I pointed at Aoife.

"Aoife O'Malley," she said. "Of the Ballywick O'Malleys."

"Ah, right," I said. "Of the Ballywick O'Malleys."

She looked at me, tearing her eyes off Aoife. "You're not from around here, eh?"

I shook my head. "How could you tell?"

"The accent's a dead giveaway," she said, then leaned closer. "The Ballywick O'Malleys are one of the top ten richest families in the country. They're in the horse business."

"The horse business?"

"Racehorses."

"And Aoife is in the racehorse business?" I asked.

"Aoife?" The woman laughed. "No, no. She was Miss Ireland a few years back. Now, she's one of them social media influencers."

I glanced around to see if Seamus had emerged from the bathroom.

"There's another of my suitcases," I said. "Thanks for the information."

"It's my pleasure," she said. "Enjoy your visit. Ireland's the best country in the world if I do say so myself."

I retrieved the suitcase from the carousel and felt a hand on my lower back.

Seamus kissed me on the cheek. "Sorry it took so long."

"No problem," I said. "I was just getting a lesson in Irish wealth."

"Irish wealth?" Seamus looked confused.

"The former Miss Ireland is here." I pointed behind us. "I'm sure you've heard of her—Aoife O'Malley? Her family is in the racehorse business."

Seamus glanced behind us quickly, grabbed a suitcase and my hand, and pulled me toward the door.

"Is everything okay?"

My heart skipped a beat. What if he knew Aoife personally? What if they had dated? If he'd dated Miss Ireland, there was no way he'd want to be with me.

"Everything's grand," he said, though his tone of voice didn't make it sound very grand. "I just want to get you to my parent's home as quickly as possible."

"Seamus?" I heard a high-pitched voice behind us.

I turned to look, but Seamus kept tugging on my arm. "Come on, keep going."

"Do you know Aoife?"

"Seamus," Aoife was running after us in her platform

5

sandals now. "Why are you running from me?"

The photographers clamored to keep up. Then I heard someone say, "Is that Seamus Healy?"

"Damn," Seamus said. "I didn't want you to find out this way."

He turned just in time for Aoife to reach us. She wrapped her arms around Seamus' neck and said, "I've missed you so much."

Cameras flashed all around us as my stomach dropped.

2

"Aoife," Seamus said when she finally let him go. "This is my girlfriend, Shayla."

Before I could steady myself, Aoife was wrapping me up in a tight hug. Her toothpick arms were stronger than they appeared. "I'm so happy to meet you. Seamus has told me all about you."

Why would Seamus have talked to his ex-girlfriend about me?

"That's good," I said, giving Seamus my best look of confusion.

"Aoife is my cousin," he said to me, then turned back to her. "And I didn't think you were going to be in town for Christmas."

"I couldn't miss it with you being here," she said.

They jabbered away—their words nearly incomprehensible. The more excited they got, the thicker their accents grew.

I wasn't paying attention, anyway.

Hadn't the woman back there said something about

Aoife's cousin being the most eligible bachelor in Ireland? The most eligible wealthy bachelor in Ireland?

A camera flash brought me back to reality.

As Aoife and Seamus caught up, the photographers captured every moment.

And they were photographing me.

It was as if I'd had blinders on my ears because, in an instant, I heard the whispers.

"Did he say she's his girlfriend?"

"The American?"

"Not possible."

"Too frumpy."

"Too plain."

"Too fat."

I sucked in a breath, trying not to tune them out. "Uh, guys," I said, my voice coming out with a squeak.

Neither of them stopped talking. How could they even understand one another when they were both talking at the same time?

"Guys?" I said louder.

Seamus glanced over at me quickly, then did a double-take. "Are you okay?"

"I think we should go," I said. My head felt like someone had injected it with helium. "Cameras."

Seamus glanced around as if he had hardly noticed. "Oh God, I'm sorry, Shay." He tucked me under his arm. "Let's get to the car."

The car waiting for us looked like something the Queen of England would ride in, not a park ranger and an American police officer.

"Aoife, did you have to bring the limo?" Seamus asked as the chauffeur loaded our suitcases in the back.

"For you and my new bestie? This hardly seems enough."

Aoife pulled out her phone and instructed me to smile. "Do you have an Instagram account? I'll tag you."

I nodded and gave her my username.

"Perfect," she said. "Now everyone will know Seamus is taken."

Seamus reached over and squeezed my hand. I watched Aoife edit the photo with quick thumbs until I didn't even recognize myself. She made my face thinner, my eyes bigger, and added what looked like a set of fake lashes.

I cringed at how much editing my photo needed.

While she busily typed away, I leaned over to Seamus and said, "When were you going to tell me you're Ireland's most eligible—and richest—bachelor?"

His cheeks flushed as he ran a hand over his hair. "I was going to tell you on the ride over," he said. "I didn't expect Aoife to pick us up."

"Why didn't you tell me before?" I asked.

"He didn't want you to be after his money," Aoife said without looking up from her phone.

Seamus blushed. "Not that I thought you would be. I just wanted you to like me for me, not for my money."

I leaned over and kissed him. "I guess you got your wish."

"Oh, that one was blurry," Aoife said, her phone held up as if she'd just taken a photo of us. "Could you do it again and just pause for a minute mid-kiss?"

Seamus shook his head. "No, thanks."

Aoife shrugged and went back to typing on her phone.

"Do you think I need to change before I meet your parents?" I whispered.

"Don't you dare change a thing," Seamus said. "I want them to see you just as I do—as the most beautiful, smart, charming woman on the planet."

I glanced down at my waist. I didn't have a fat roll spilling over the top of my pants, but I still felt fat. Especially after the whispers at the airport and Aoife's photo modifications.

I tried to shake the thought away. Seamus had fallen in love with me when I'd been at my heaviest. He loved me for me. It didn't matter what anyone else said.

"Please tell me you don't live in a castle," I said.

Seamus laughed. "I don't live in a castle."

"He doesn't," Aoife said without taking her eyes off her screen. "But we do."

"Aoife and her brother, Killian, still live with their parents on the family compound," Seamus teased.

"Family compound?" I asked.

"It sounds worse than it is," Seamus said. "Our grandparents left a large piece of property for their three children—my mother, Aoife's father, and our Uncle Alabaster. Each of them was given a sum of money to build a house."

Aoife held up a hand to correct him.

"Correction, Aoife's father wanted the castle, so they gave him the primary residence on the estate while the other two got cash to build the home they chose on their piece of the property." Seamus waited for Aoife to nod in agreement before he continued. "My parents built a home—"

"A mansion," Aoife corrected.

"A large home," Seamus said. "Uncle Alabaster went with more of a cottage since it's just him."

"And your family races horses?" I asked.

"Not us personally. My mother owns a team, and she breeds racehorses," Seamus said.

"What do Aoife's parents do? Are they in the racehorse business too?"

"They sold their shares to my mother ages ago," Seamus said.

"My parents get by on their investments," Aoife said. "Someday, they'll move into a smaller place, and I'll get the castle. I want to turn it into an upscale B&B. It'll be amazing. I've been working on plans for ages."

Seamus looked at her and frowned but said nothing.

"Oh, and Killian doesn't live at home anymore," she said. "He moved to the city a few weeks ago."

"Your parents must be delighted," Seamus said. "At least one of their grown children has decided to strike out on their own rather than waiting around for a damp old castle."

"Hey," Aoife said, kicking Seamus with her platform sandal. "They were actually quite distraught about it. Though, I don't know why. They won't tell me, but I heard them arguing. Killian is always so mean to them. I would have kicked him out ages ago."

"Will Killian be around for the holidays?" Seamus asked.

"If he knows you're here, he will be," Aoife said. "This'll be the first time he's been home since he left in a tizzy."

The driver took a sharp turn into a long driveway. I tried to see out the tinted windows as we passed through a large wrought-iron gate attached to a tall stone wall. Trees lined the drive to the house.

Or as Aoife had correctly described it—the mansion.

3

I hadn't brushed up on my manners. Heck, I didn't even know what the proper manners were in Ireland.

Seamus grabbed my hand. "Don' be worrin', they're gonna luv ya."

I was almost certain his accent had gotten thicker since we'd landed at the airport.

The minute the chauffeur opened our door, two people— Seamus' mother and father, presumably—rushed down the stone stairway to greet us.

His mother wore riding pants and a tight-fitting button-down. Her salt and pepper hair was pulled back into a sleek low bun, and she wore almost no makeup. She wrapped her arms so tightly around Seamus's neck, he had a hard time speaking.

His father and I stood awkwardly, waiting for Seamus to introduce us.

"Da, Mam, this is Shayla," Seamus finally said.

His mother released her son and opened her arms to me.

My mom wasn't a big hugger, but I was. Opposites again.

I soaked in the warm hug. His mother smelled like expensive perfume and horses.

"You may call me Mam or Gráinne," she said. "But please, nothing more formal than that."

Gráinne was another name Seamus had gone over with me. It sounded Grawn-yuh.

"Thank you," I said. "It's lovely to meet you."

Seamus and his father embraced for a quick second, and his father extended a hand to me. "I am Donal."

I shook his hand. "It's a pleasure."

"The pleasure is all mine." He gave me a friendly smile.

"Are me mam and da here?" Aoife asked.

"They're inside," Gráinne said. "As is Killian."

Seamus positively lit up. "Killian's here?" He grabbed my hand and pulled me toward the stairs leading to the massive front entry doors. The home was a light yellow, and the doors were made of dark wood. "I can't wait for you to meet him. Killian is like a brother to me."

The entry was a brighter shade of yellow—almost a cream —with a staircase that wound its way up to a second level. I could only imagine how many times they'd had to repaint the white banister from Seamus sliding down.

Where the house looked like a mansion from the outside, it was far cozier inside.

"He's in the kitchen," Gráinne said with a laugh.

"Course he is," Seamus said, tugging me along with him.

I didn't have much time to observe the surroundings as we made our way down the hallway by a large sitting room on the left and a few doors on the right into the sweetest eat-in kitchen I'd ever seen.

A small round table sat next to a roaring fireplace with a massive painting of Santa and Rudolph above. The actual kitchen was through a large archway. Its muted blue-green cupboards and large wooden peg handles gave off so many homely vibes, I considered asking Gráinne for the paint color right then and there.

Sitting with his back to us at the large island breakfast bar was who I assumed to be Killian.

"Alright, mucker?" Seamus said.

I gasped.

Gráinne laughed. "It's a term of endearment, love."

I smiled at her, relieved, and watched as Killian stood from his stool. He was at least a head taller than Seamus with dark black hair and inquisitive eyes. But when he smiled, his face changed from haunting to downright friendly.

"It's about time you came back," Killian said, holding his arms open for Seamus.

"What's the craic?" Seamus said, embracing his teary-eyed cousin.

"Divil a bit," Killian said. "Nothing much."

They separated but held each other by the shoulders. "That's not what yer sister's been saying." Seamus glanced back. But Aoife hadn't joined us. She was probably off looking for her parents.

"What's she on about now?"

"Said you moved out of the castle."

"She'd be right," Killian said. "But let's not bring it up 'round me mam and da. They be havin' a wee bit of issue with it."

Seamus nodded once. "Meet me girl." He reached for my hand. "This is Shayla Murphy. Shayla, this is Killian."

"Pleasure," Killian said, shaking my hand, though his smile faltered a bit when his gaze met mine. "Seamus tells me yer a guard?"

"A police officer," Seamus corrected. "Same difference."

"I understand you carry a gun?" Killian said.

Was his hesitation with me because I was an American police officer who carried a gun? "I do."

"And yeh know how to be usin' it?"

"I've had extensive firearms training," I said. "My mom was a police officer, so I grew up around firearms."

"Sounds dangerous," Killian said.

"Only if you're not careful," I said, keeping my tone light. "I hope never to have to use my firearm."

"Did you bring it with you?" Killian asked.

I shook my head. "Nope. No guns here."

Killian nodded in approval.

"Now that that's settled," Donal said, laying an arm across Gráinne's shoulder. "Shall we let these two get cozy?"

"That sounds lovely," Gráinne said, smiling up at him, then turning back to us. "And as soon as you've taken a rest, we can have some tea and a chat."

How was this woman so warm? The only other woman I'd felt so instantly comfortable around was my best friend Rylie's mom.

Seamus squeezed my hand, and we started to walk away, but the sound of a door slamming drew all of our attention.

"Uncle Alabaster, he's only just gotten here. Please, don't do this." Aoife's voice was almost afraid.

She followed a little white-haired man with deep frown lines and an even deeper voice. "Shut yer gob yeh eejit. I ain't fixin' to hurt the lad. Even if he is deservin'."

Aoife looked like she'd been slapped in the face as tears welled in her eyes.

Gráinne rushed to her side. "That wasn't nice of you, Alabaster."

"She tried to stop me from seein' me nephew." Alabaster said. "He owes me an explanation."

I looked over at Seamus, anxiety welling up inside me. But Seamus was looking at Killian.

"Why don't we take this outside," Killian said. "No need arguing with Seamus' lady here."

Alabaster narrowed his eyes at Killian, then turned to us. "The prodigal son returns, I see." He let out a kind of snort and turned away, not bothering to introduce himself to me. "Let's go."

He reached up, grabbed Killian by the ear, and pulled him toward the door.

"Uncle, please," Killian said as he followed, hunched over. "I said I was sorry."

"Go with them," Gráinne said to Donal. "Make sure Alabaster doesn't hurt Killian."

Donal sighed. "Perhaps Killian deserves what's coming to him."

Aoife cried harder, and Gráinne shot Donal a fierce glare.

Donal didn't apologize but simply followed the other two outside.

"I'm so sorry yeh had to see that," Gráinne said, wrapping an arm around Aoife's shoulder. "I'm sure Alabaster will show better manners tonight at the party."

"A Party, Mam?" Seamus asked. "I didn't know about a party."

"Just a few friends," Gráinne said. "'Twas your da's idea. If ya want to be angry at someone, take it up with him."

Seamus sighed. "I suppose we better get some rest."

"We'll see you 'round later," Gráinne said to me. "I can't wait to introduce you to all my friends. They're gonna love you."

I wasn't sure they would, but I smiled nonetheless. "I look forward to it."

4

Seamus led me up a set of stairs off the kitchen rather than the ones we'd gone past in the entry. We wound down a hall painted a beautiful cream color with white baseboards and molding to a bedroom with a hand-painted sign that said, "Seamus Room. Stay Out or ELSE." It was completely out of place with the chicness of the house, but it was cute that his parents still kept it up.

"Why would you have a sign on your door like that when you were an only child?" I laughed.

"I might have been my parents' only child, but living so close to Killian and Aoife, they were practically siblings. Plus, a couple of the staff had children. We all grew up together. They called us the Fab Five."

I expected to see a teenage boy's bedroom when he opened the door, but instead, it was a beautifully decorated guest suite. Sure, sports team posters hung around on the walls, but they were framed and signed—presumably by the players.

The curtains were a dark plaid that matched the pillow-cases on the otherwise white bedding. A large bookshelf took up an entire wall with various trophies interspersed between books.

Our luggage had already been brought up and was waiting neatly on stands.

I sat in an oversized chair and looked up at the man I loved. "I can't believe this is your family home. That this is the bedroom you grew up in."

"I'm sorry I wasn't more upfront," he said. "Plus, it's not like this is my money. It's my parents'. I've always wanted to be a self-made man."

"Your uncle called you the prodigal son," I said. "Does that mean you ran away to be wild and crazy?"

Seamus laughed. "Not in the least. I didn't run away. I chose to leave. I got an opportunity to become a Prairie City summie. I thought it would be a simple summer job, but I really enjoyed it."

"Have you ever thought about coming back?" It was a loaded question. I was half-tempted to explain that I didn't care either way and that it wouldn't influence our relationship, but a stronger part of me told me to wait for the answer.

"Doesn't everyone think about going home from time to time?" Seamus asked.

I shook my head. "Not everyone."

He sighed. "I'm sorry. That was insensitive. I'm just tired and—"

I stood up and wrapped my arms around his waist. "It's okay. I understand. If this were my home, I'd want to come back too."

He kissed me on my forehead. "Should we get some shut-eye before the big party?"

"About this party, is it a fancy party? I only brought along one dress," I said. "And I planned on using that for your Christmas party."

"Sounds like what you need is some retail therapy," he said. "And before you say anything, mam will insist on buying anything you need. So let her. It's one of the joys in her life—buying things for people."

I wanted to object, but I was too excited. Who wouldn't want an all-expenses-paid shopping spree in Ireland? "I suppose if I have to."

Seamus laughed. "There's my girl." He tilted my chin up, so our gazes met. "Have I told you today just how beautiful you are?"

I held back the rebuttal sitting on the tip of my tongue. "Thank you. You're pretty handsome yourself."

"Bed?"

"Bed."

We might not have gone straight to sleep, but what we did helped us sleep a bit more soundly.

A tap at the door woke me up. Seamus was no longer in bed. I wiped drool from the corner of my mouth and smoothed my hair down. "Yes?"

"Miss Murphy? I'm here to help you get ready." A woman's voice said from the other side of the door.

I got to my feet as quickly as I could, threw on a luxurious robe that had been placed next to the bed while I was sleeping, and opened the door. The woman was probably in her mid-sixties with dark red hair and a slender build.

"I am Magella," she said.

"Hi Magella," I said. "I'm Shayla—Seamus' girlfriend."

"Oh yes, I've heard all about you," she said. Her accent wasn't at all hard to understand. "Would you like my help getting ready for the party? I can draw you a bath, steam your dress, and assist you with your hair and makeup."

Whether Seamus had specifically set this up for me, or this was the norm, I wasn't sure. But either way, I didn't mind.

"That would be wonderful," I said. "Thank you."

"Ah, you don't need to be thanking me. It's me job." She winked. "But I'd probably do it for you even it wasn't."

In the attached bathroom, Magella ran a steaming hot bath with floral-scented bath salts. "Take your time in there. The party's not for another few hours."

"Thank you," I said, feeling like a broken record. I'd thanked her at least fifteen times since she'd arrived at my door.

"Did you want me to steam your dress while you bathe?"

"That would be wonderful. It's hanging in the closet." I hadn't wanted to leave it on the bed, and her think me too presumptuous, but I also didn't want her to have to go rummaging through my suitcase. Thankfully, the dress wasn't too terribly wrinkled.

She closed the door and left me to my glorious bath. I almost didn't want to leave, but eventually, the water got cold, and my skin was wrinkly.

When I emerged, Magella had a tray of tea and small pastries set out for me. "Something to tide you over."

My stomach growled, and we both laughed.

"While you have a bite, I'll do your hair," she said.

I sat in a chair positioned in front of a full-length mirror I suspected had been brought in especially for me.

"Where's Seamus?" I asked.

"He's getting ready with Killian," she said. "Tis good to see those two together again. It's been ages."

"Seamus said it had been a while since he'd been back home."

"They were inseparable growing up," she said. "It wasn't until Seamus left for America that they grew distant."

"I suppose growing up will do that to you," I said.

"It was good for Killian, though." She ran a comb through my hair. "I don't know if he'd have ever grown up without Seamus leaving him."

"I take it you've been here a long time?"

"Since I was fresh out of school," she said. "They took me in, gave me a home, a job, and a place for my daughter to grow up. The O'Malleys are good folks."

"You have a daughter?" I asked.

She stopped combing and pulled out a smartphone in a designer case. "This is her. She's married and has her own family now. She'll be at the party, though."

The photo showed a woman who looked like a younger version of her mother—dark red hair, pretty smile—standing next to a tall man with a raven-colored afro. Their two daughters had their auburn afros pulled back into poufs on top of their heads.

"Gorgeous family," I said. "Will they all be coming tonight?"

"The wee ones will stay with their other grandma," she said. "Normally, they would stay with me, as I'm not one for big parties, but Gráinne insisted I come. Both Clara and Edward will be in attendance."

"I look forward to meeting them," I said.

She returned her phone to the pocket of her pants and continued combing. "You have beautiful hair. It's so thick and silky."

"It's probably my best quality," I said. "And likely the reason Seamus was interested in me at all. I was quite a bit larger than I am now when we first met."

"Seamus was never one to pick a woman for her looks— not that you're bad looking, mind you," she added the last part quickly. "But after his near-miss, he learned a valuable lesson in love. I suspect he loves you because he can trust you."

"His near-miss?" I asked.

"I suppose I should say his last near-miss." She laughed. "There was a string of them."

"As in women?" I knew he'd been engaged once in Ireland and again right after arriving in America, but I didn't realize he'd dated so much.

"Lots of them. Beauties, they were." She pulled out a hairdryer and talked over the noise. "And that last one was a doozie."

I wasn't certain whether Magella knew about his engagement in the States, so I was sure to tread carefully. "I think he told me about her. They met in college, right?"

"They got engaged the last week of college, but they met when they were kids. She lived here growing up."

"Clara?" I asked.

She laughed. "No, no, no. Not my Clara. I made certain she stayed away from the O'Malley boys. Romantically, at least. Couldn't separate the kids, though."

"She was one of the Fab Five?"

Magella smiled. "I haven't heard the term Fab Five in forever. Clara, Aoife, Killian, Seamus, and Nuala."

"Is Nuala the near miss?" I asked.

"That she is," Magella said.

"Can you tell me about her?" I asked.

In the mirror, I could see Magella contemplating whether to give me details. "I suppose you'll find out tonight, anyway."

"Tonight?"

"I probably shouldn't tell you this, but Nuala will be in attendance at the party."

5

Nuala was a beautiful name.

"Can you tell me about her?" I asked. "Just so I'm prepared."

"There's nothing I can tell you about Nuala to prepare you for her," Magella said. "She's a right terror, she is."

"Who are her parents?"

Magella had moved on from blow-drying to curling my hair. "They don't work here anymore. They retired years ago, then divorced. They used to do all the gardening. Rose—Nuala's mother—has a nice flower business in town now."

I sat up straighter. "I look forward to meeting Nuala."

"That's me girl," Magella said. "I forgot you're a police officer. No way a fashion model would intimidate an officer of the law."

I felt a twinge of nausea in my stomach. Fashion model?

"Now, shall we work on your makeup?"

Magella made me look like a fairy tale princess. My makeup was flawless and natural, my hair was smoothed into an elegant updo, and my dress was—well—the only dress I brought, so I'd have to be okay with it. At least it was sparkly.

"Gráinne wanted to offer you this tonight as well." Magella opened an old velvet necklace box that held a breathtaking emerald and diamond necklace and matching teardrop earrings.

I gasped.

"Don't be worrying. I won't snap your hand in the box if you want to touch it," she said. "Not like in that American movie about the prostitute."

"Pretty Woman?"

"That's the one." She pulled the necklace off the silk fabric inside the box. "May I?"

I turned and let her affix it around my neck. "I feel more like Cinderella than Vivian from Pretty Woman."

She smiled. "Let's get these in your ears and get you downstairs before the guests arrive."

The walk downstairs was both too long and too short. Walking in heels had always been something I did well, but the floors were slippery. When I reached the bottom of the stairs in one piece, Seamus came around the corner looking more handsome—and richer—than I'd ever seen.

"Wow," I said. "You clean up nice."

He kissed me square on the lips as Magella excused herself. Tingles went from my lips to my knees. He was the best kisser I'd ever laid lips on.

"You're stunning," he said. "I can't wait to show you off."

"Did you know your ex-fiancée is going to be here?" I asked.

"A lot of people will be here," he said. "But I'm here with you. Only you."

I told myself he was telling the truth. Why would he lie to me? He brought me here from across the ocean to meet his family. If that wasn't commitment, I didn't know what was.

I nodded once.

"The elders are having a pre-party meeting in the den," he said. "Me mam is probably telling Uncle Alabaster to keep his hands to himself and my Uncle Geoffrey not to burden the guests with his newest money-making scheme."

"Where are Aoife and Killian?" I asked.

"Aoife was still getting ready from what Auntie Shannon said, and Killian should be here any moment with his new squeeze." He leaned into me and kissed my neck. "Mmmm . . . maybe we should skip the party and go back upstairs."

"Ah, get a room," Killian's voice boomed.

Following him into the room was a tall woman with a face so skinny, her cheeks were sunken in, and her cheekbones protruded. She wore a long sheer silver gown with jewels strategically placed to cover the bits that would be inappropriate to show. It had a v-neck to her navel and a slit to her hip.

"Nuala?" Seamus said. "Is that you?"

"Tis me," she said, her voice frail like a bird. "Good to see you again, Seamus."

Seamus gaped at Killian.

"I been meaning to tell you, but the timing was always off," Killian said. "Nuala and I have been seeing each other for a few months now."

"Seven," Nuala said, wrapping her bony arm through Killian's. "Best seven months of my life."

Killian puffed up his chest.

They were putting on a show for Seamus.

"It's a pleasure to meet you, Nuala," I said, stepping

between Seamus and Killian. "I'm Shayla, Seamus' girlfriend from the United States."

Nuala looked me up and down. She probably weighed less than a hundred pounds and was easily five inches taller than me, but that didn't mean she was as beautiful as I'd expected her to be.

"I have a hard time believing Seamus would take up with a girl like you," Nuala said.

I took a step back, and Seamus grabbed my hand.

"What d'ya mean by that?" Seamus asked.

Her mouth went into a strained smile. "Oh, I'm just coddin' ya." She opened her arms. "Come here and give me a hug."

Was she asking me for a hug or Seamus?

Seamus didn't let go of my hand.

"For old time's sake," she said. "It's just a hug."

Seamus looked back at me.

"Need your girl's permission to give someone a hug, do ya?" Nuala's gentle voice had a way of cutting straight to the core.

I nodded, and Seamus gave her a quick hug, patting her on the back twice as she nuzzled her face into his hair.

He pulled away and glared at her.

"Right," she said, stepping back to Killian, who looked like he couldn't have cared less who she hugged. "Now, what were the geezers fighting about in there?"

"As in our parents?" Seamus asked. "I didn't know they were fighting. I thought they were just going over the ground rules of the evening."

Killian shrugged. "Sounded important. Probably about money."

Seamus sighed. "Has it been bad?"

"How should I know?" Killian said. "I got out of here as soon as I could. The bickering was getting old, you know? I'd rather not get anything than get something I have to fight for."

"Agreed," Seamus said.

Nuala frowned at Killian.

If Seamus had dodged a bullet with her, presumably because she was only after his money, wouldn't Killian know she might only be after his money, too?

I stopped my train of thought. The police officer in me was coming out. Not that I was an investigator or anything. Not like my mom.

"That's enough fighting," Alabaster burst from a doorway down the hall and yelled at whoever was still in the room. "Whoever proposes first gets the ring. How 'bout that?"

He turned in the direction opposite us stomped off toward the back of the house.

Killian and Seamus looked like they'd just seen a ghost.

The ghost of Christmas commitment.

Gráinne and Donal walked out of the room, followed by who I assumed were Killian's parents.

"He's just doing this because he thinks he can," Killian's mom—a large woman wearing a scowl and a lot of makeup— said. Her dress was blush-colored and tight in all the wrong places.

"What kind of malarkey are you spewing?" Killian's dad said. "He thinks he can because he can. He controls it. He controls everything."

"That's enough from you two," Gráinne said. "Hello kids."

Killian's parents both whipped around to find us standing there.

"How much of that did yeh hear?" Killian's dad asked.

"We just walked in," Seamus said, putting a smile on his face. "This is Shayla."

"It's a pleasure to meet you, Shayla. I'm Shannon."

Killian's mom didn't look thrilled to meet me. "And this is me husband, Geoffrey."

"Me brother," Gráinne said. "He and Alabaster gave me a run for me money as kids."

"She practically raised us," Geoffrey said. "Me more than Alabaster. He always had a bit of a stick up his arse."

"Geoffrey," Gráinne said. "Be nice, will ya?"

He threw his hands in the air and walked past us. "Nice meetin' ya."

Shannon followed. "We'll see you at the party."

"Was Uncle Al talking about a ring?" Nuala asked Gráinne.

"What's it to you?" Gráinne asked, her kind demeanor slipping. She wore a purple dress with light swishy fabric belted just below her chest. Her shoes were pointed-toe heels in a mustard color.

Nuala shrugged. "Just wonderin'."

"He was talking about giving a friend a ring," Donal said. "On the telly. That's why he stormed out. Had something he needed to take care of."

Gráinne nodded as if that was the end of the conversation. "Oh, Shayla," she said. "You look brilliant in me mother's necklace and earrings. I want you to have them."

I gasped.

Nuala gasped.

Seamus beamed.

"I—no—I couldn't." I reached up and touched the gorgeous gems hanging around my neck.

"I won't be takin' no for an answer," she said. "They look perfect on you. Now, how about we greet our guests?"

"No one's here yet, mam," Seamus said.

The doorbell rang, and Gráinne smirked. "You were sayin'?"

Seamus, Donal, and I laughed.

6

"Jaysus, Mary, and Joseph," Aoife said when she barged into the kitchen about a half-hour into the party looking svelte in black pants with small white polka dots that came to her natural waist and a ruffled white blouse. "Don't tell me Killian's with that little traitor."

"Looks like it," Seamus said. "Apparently, they've been dating a while."

Aoife wrapped an arm around my neck. "She's absolutely awful. What she did to our poor Seamus—"

"Is not a topic of discussion for tonight," Seamus said. "Tonight, we're celebrating Shayla."

A clinking came from the den. "Can I have everyone's attention, please?" Killian's voice rose over the crowd.

"What's he on about now?" Aoife said.

We followed her into the den. The lighting was perfect—low enough to make it cozy but also flattering, making the jewelry hanging from the women's necks and ears sparkle along with their eyes.

"As you may or may not know," Killian said, "Nuala and I have been dating a few months now."

"Seven," Nuala said, pride written all over her face.

"And we are thrilled now that we're finally together in Dublin," Killian continued. "My business is taking off, and Nuala just became the face of one of the biggest modeling agencies in Ireland."

Nuala turned and glared at Aoife. I suspected if there weren't so many people around, one of them might have stuck a tongue out.

I glanced at the other guests. Clara and her husband, Edward, stood near the door. Clara wore a tiered pink dress that looked like it was made of lace. Her hair was in a beautiful braid that flowed over her shoulder.

Alabaster and Gráinne stood together near the piano. Donal wasn't present. Nor were Shannon or Geoffrey.

If Killian was about to propose, why wouldn't he have waited for his parents to be there?

The conversation from before popped into my head quicker than he could pop the question.

The ring.

"I thought about doing this a thousand different ways," Killian said.

"Sure he did," Aoife mumbled to Seamus and me. She probably had the same thought as I had.

"But tonight just seemed right with all of our friends and family here," Killian said.

"Their friends and family?" Seamus scoffed. "His parents aren't even here."

"Are hers?" I asked.

"By the bookcases," Aoife said.

We both looked at where Aoife motioned. A blonde woman and dark-haired man stood in the shadows, frowns on their faces. The woman wore a tight-fitting black satin one-piece pantsuit with billowing straps that hung down her arms.

Killian dropped to a knee and took Nuala's hand in his. "I love you very much."

"I love you too," Nuala said, but when she did, I could have sworn she glanced up at Seamus.

He dropped his gaze to the floor.

Killian turned, looked at Alabaster, and whispered, "The ring?"

Alabaster's face flushed. "I'm sorry, what did ye say?"

"I'm proposing," Killian said. "You said whoever proposed first got the ring, yeah?"

I smiled at being right about the ring.

"Yeh heard that, did ya?" Alabaster spat. "Did yeh hear the rest of me conversation?"

"I—uh—" Killian looked confused.

Nuala looked ready to burst into tears. Happy or sad—it wasn't clear.

"You'll only get that ring over me dead body," Alabaster said. "Everyone knows it's Seamus' ring for the taking. Tonight was supposed to be his night, but yeh heard me talk about the ring, and yeh decided to make a right fool of yourself. Shame be on you."

Alabaster turned and stormed out the door.

Killian rose from his knee.

"Wait? Aren't you still proposing?" Nuala asked.

Killian didn't give her the courtesy of an answer. He followed his uncle, leaving Nuala in a puddle of tears.

"What an absolute shite show," Aoife said, her tone gleeful. "He never wanted to marry her. He just wanted that silly ring."

"Why?" I asked.

"It's worth a small fortune," Aoife said, taking her voice to a whisper.

"And with Uncle Alabaster changing his will, none of us know what we'll be gettin'." Seamus frowned.

"Is he sick?" I asked. "Is that why he's changing his will?"

"Not at all," Seamus said. "Mam and Da said he's been talking about this for a while but finally pulled the trigger."

"How did he say he changed it?" Aoife asked.

"Don't know." Seamus shrugged. "But it doesn't look good for Killian."

"Why would Killian have a piece of Alabaster's will?" I asked.

"Uncle Alabaster has no children," Seamus said. "And our parents all have their portions from the estate. Uncle Alabaster always said he'd leave his wealth to his favorite nieces and nephews."

Seamus smiled at Aoife, and she smiled back, though her smile was hesitant. "Do you think he'll remove Killian from that list?"

"Hell, if I know," Seamus said. "The ring might be a one-off."

"So? Are you gonna propose now?" Aoife asked.

"I'd rather eat my own boogers," Seamus said, then quickly added. "Not that I don't want to propose. I just want to when the time is right. I don't want to rush it. And I definitely don't want to propose the same night Killian does. Or almost did."

I put a hand on his arm. "It's okay. You don't have to explain anything to me."

Seamus sighed.

"You're too sweet for me teeth. I'm gonna get cavities just listenin' to ya," Aoife said. "I need to catch up with Clara. Maybe that hunky hubby of hers has a brother."

"I'm sorry yeh had to see that," Seamus said. "Killian's gotten greedy in his old age. Thinks he's entitled to every-thin'. I'm guessin' he gets it from his mam. She probably put him up to the proposal."

"I feel terrible for Nuala," I said. "Maybe someone should check on her."

She'd practically faded away into the crowd, and—as far as I could tell—no one had gone after her.

"It's probably best if it's not me," Seamus said.

"I'll go," I said.

"You're a saint." Seamus pulled me close to him, wrapping his arms around my waist, and kissed me. "I love you."

"I love you too." I smiled, then walked out the door and down the hallway leading to the back of the house.

When I passed a closed door, I heard what sounded like someone sobbing.

I tried to turn the handle, but it was locked.

Just before I knocked, something shattered on the other side of the door.

"You sleazy bastard," a woman's voice yelled.

"Don't do it," a man said. I couldn't be certain, but it sounded like Alabaster.

Another crash came from the opposite side of the door.

I knocked. "Is everything okay in there?"

The door swung open, and the woman who had been standing in the shadows before—Nuala's mother—came huffing out. "It was self-defense. He assaulted me. He needs to be brought up on charges."

Did she know I was a police officer? "Uh, I—"

She huffed and stomped away.

I turned to glance inside the room. Alabaster lay on the carpet. His eyes rolled back in his head.

7

I rushed to his side and checked for breathing.

If she had killed him, we needed to stop her quickly.

Thankfully, Alabaster's chest rose slightly.

When I slid two fingers onto his neck, he had a strong pulse.

His eyes fluttered open. "What happened?"

"A woman said you attacked her," I said.

"Attacked her, huh?" He chuckled a bit. "She mistook my intentions." He pointed toward the ceiling.

I glanced up to find what looked like real mistletoe hanging from a spot in the low-hanging rafters.

"How about a kiss for luck?" He smiled up at me.

I leaned down and kissed his forehead. "How's that?"

"You're Seamus' girl, right?"

"That I am," I said, helping him come to a sit. "Why are you down here?"

He pointed to the shattered pieces of glass around him. "I hit the deck when she threw that at me."

"Why'd she throw it at you? Did you try to kiss her

without her consent?" I thought back to what Seamus had said about the adults going over Alabaster, keeping his hands to himself.

"Nah, it wasn't like that," Alabaster said. "She followed me in here and made a holy show of herself, insisting we should kiss under the mistletoe. When I said no, she took offense and started throwing things."

I wasn't sure I bought his story, but I let it go. It wasn't my place to investigate. If she wanted to file a complaint, she could do so with the Gardaí. "Do you feel you can stand?"

"Maybe with a wee bit of help from a beautiful young lady," he said.

I eased him to his feet, careful to stay steady on my heels.

"Alabaster, what happened?" Gráinne rushed in and instantly saw the glass all over the floor.

"I'll pay for it," Alabaster said.

"I'm not worried about the vases," Gráinne said. "Why is Shayla helping you up from the floor?"

"I slipped is all." Alabaster gave me a look that told me to go along with what he said. I figured I would until it felt wrong not to. "Seamus is a lucky lad to have such a kind mot. Killian could use a bit of his sense." He glanced around as he said this.

I wasn't sure what a mot was but figured it had something to do with me.

"Let's not start comparing the boys again," Gráinne said. "Thank you for helping him, Shayla."

"It was no problem at all," I said. "I should probably get back to Seamus. You be careful, Mr. O'Malley."

"Me father was Mr. O'Malley," Alabaster said. "Please, call me Al."

Gráinne gave him a funny look, then turned back to me and shrugged.

"Al it is," I said.

When I started back out of the room, I remembered why I'd come down the hallway in the first place—I had been looking for Nuala.

I checked the bathroom next to the study and the kitchen but didn't see her.

It wasn't until I was on the back porch that I smelled the cigarette smoke and followed the scent to find Nuala with mascara streaked down her face. "What do you want?"

"Just thought I'd check on you," I said. "That was pretty brutal back there."

"He wanted the ring." She took a long drag, the embers lighting up the tip of her pointy nose. "I knew that. I just didn't think he'd use me to get it."

"How did you know he wanted the ring?" I asked. "Did you know he was going to propose?"

"He talks about that stupid ring all the time. It's hideous but worth a fortune," Nuala said. "I wouldn't have been caught dead wearing it. I tried to find Alabaster to get him to reconsider, but he was locked in a room with one of his many girlfriends. It's a wonder he doesn't have an heir to leave his fortune to."

I didn't respond. She didn't need to know what had actually happened in that locked room. Or that Alabaster was with her mother.

"Can I get you anything?" I finally asked.

"Why are you bein' nice to me?" Nuala asked. "Don't you know what I did to your boyfriend?"

"It doesn't matter," I lied. "That's in the past."

"I heard he ran off to America and proposed to the first girl he met. Is that true?"

I shrugged, but she probably couldn't see that in the dark. "He was engaged to someone."

"Typical Seamus, rushing into things. You would have thought he would have learned."

My insides twisted. We had been dating more than a year, and we'd barely spoken about marriage. "Maybe he has."

"You keep telling yourself that." She laughed and threw the cigarette butt on the ground, not bothering to stomp on it. "Maybe the reason he hasn't proposed is that he doesn't want to marry you. He heard what Alabaster said about the ring. You'd think he'd have already gotten down on his knee."

She brushed past me, walking back into the house.

I stepped on her cigarette butt and sighed. I could feel the pity party rising in my mind, starting with the question—what if she was right?

I pushed the feelings away and my shoulders back. Nuala didn't know me. Didn't know Seamus anymore. He was a different person—a grown man. My grown man.

I marched back inside.

"How'd that go?" Seamus said with a cheeky smirk on his face.

"About as good as you'd expect," I said. "I think she's okay."

"Let's get in the den and introduce you around." Seamus squeezed my hand in his. "The guests are gettin' restless seein' as they came here to meet you."

I followed along behind him, doing my best to appear confident and charming. Just like my mom had always instructed.

Her voice rang in my ear—you could be so much more if you just tried.

More confident. More athletic. More everything.

And—as much as I hated it every time she mentioned the mores—she was right. I only needed to apply myself.

"Seamus, I'm so happy to see you," Clara said, kissing him on the cheek. "This is Edward."

"It's brilliant to meet you," Edward said in an English accent. "Clara has spoken highly of you."

"Yeh didn't tell me he was English," Seamus laughed. "I guess I'll give yeh a pass."

Edward and Clara laughed too.

"And you must be Shayla," Clara said. "It's lovely to meet you."

She wrapped me in a big hug.

"It's nice to meet you too," I said. "I met your mother earlier. She's responsible for my makeover."

"Don't listen to her," Seamus said. "She's a knockout with or without the makeup and fancy clothes."

I smiled at him. "Thank you."

"Young love," Clara said. "Do you remember when we were first in love?"

Edward pulled Clara closer to him. "How could I forget?"

She giggled.

"Edward, I hear you're a solicitor?" Seamus asked. "Sounds terribly boring."

"It pays the bills," Edward said, taking his focus off his bride. "I followed in my father's footsteps."

"Family business?" Seamus said. "I know how that goes."

"Do yeh now?" Clara put her hands on her hips and stared him down. "'Cause last I knew, yeh ran at the slightest mention of taking over the business."

I did my best to keep my facial expressions neutral as the whispers from the airport came back to me.

"I didn't run because o'that," Seamus said. "I didn't run at all. They offered me the summer position in America. You know that."

"How many summers ago? I suspected you'd be back before now," Clara said, punching him in the arm. "Some of us missed you, yeh know?"

Seamus rubbed his arm, acting like it hurt more than it

probably had. "I'm sorry, Clara. I never meant to abandon you." His voice was sweet. "It's a good thing you found this English fellow to help you cope."

She laughed and wiped a tear from her eye.

Edward looked at them a bit suspiciously.

Should I worry too?

Magella said she'd warned her daughter not to date Seamus and Killian. But had Clara heeded that warning?

8

As the night went on, drinks flowed, and lips loosened. Killian and Nuala seemed to be back in good spirits. Even Uncle Alabaster—Al—seemed to be enjoying himself. Maybe even a bit too much.

"Are your Uncle Geoffrey and Aunt Shannon coming?" I asked Seamus as he handed me a pint of Guinness.

"Seems they had more important business to take care of tonight," Seamus said. "I'm sorry, love."

"It's okay. I'm glad I got to meet them earlier," I said with a smile. "Your family and friends are wonderful."

"Yeah, they are." He wrapped an arm around my shoulders and smiled at the group of people in front of him.

"I'm impressed," a voice said from behind us.

We turned to find a very rosy-cheeked Al.

"Why's that Uncle Alabaster?" Seamus asked.

"I figured you'd get down on your knee, too," Al said. "Try your hand at getting the ring."

Seamus blushed. "Don't be needing a ring."

Al quirked an eyebrow up, then hooked an arm around my waist and pulled me toward him.

I yelped in surprise.

"You better snatch this fine thing up before someone else does," Al said.

I took a deep breath. The last thing I needed to do was cause a scene by pushing an old guy off me. Or worse—hitting him. But that's what my instincts were yelling for me to do.

"He doesn't need to snatch me up," I said. "I'm firmly committed to our relationship."

"Let her go, Uncle," Seamus warned. "Yer ossified."

"What if I don't let her go?" Al slurred. "I'm the controlling stake in this family. You wouldn't dare try to hurt me."

"If you hurt Shayla, I'll have no choice but to return the favor," Seamus said. "Let her go."

"I have no intentions of causing her pain. But a sweet girl like her wouldn't dare deny me another kiss under the mistletoe, would she?" He was directing his question at me.

I glanced up and saw mistletoe above our heads.

"Another kiss?" Seamus asked.

Everyone was staring at us by now.

"It was a kiss on the forehead when he fell," I said. "And I think that was quite enough."

Where was the nice guy I'd talked to in the study?

Alabaster tightened his grip on me and planted his lips firmly on mine, his tongue squirming around, trying to squeeze between my lips.

My arms acted before my brain could tell them not to. I pushed him so hard he tumbled onto his backside. Thankfully, we were far enough from any furniture he didn't hit his head.

"Oh my gosh," I said, reaching to help him up. "I'm so sorry."

"Don't be sorry," Gráinne said, appearing next to me. "He deserved every bit of that push."

Much to my surprise, Alabaster's lips—the same lips that had been on mine just seconds before—parted into a smile. "Suppose I did." He took my hand and pulled back up to a stand.

I stepped back, careful to avoid being caught by him again.

Seamus stepped between Alabaster and me. "Why're yeh acting the maggot? You apologize to Shayla right now."

Alabaster stood a bit taller. "Big lad, are we? Ya dosser. Run away from home at the slightest mention of responsibility only to come back with your American mot. Yeh came back for the ring, didn't ya?"

"I told you before, I don't need your stupid ring," Seamus said. "I don't need anything from you. You can keep holding your money over Killian and Aoife's heads, but I have no use for it. Donate it all to a feline shelter for all I care."

Alabaster's face paled. "Well, that's good because I just had my will redone."

"I didn't think we were going to be telling the youngins about that," Gráinne said.

"Don't know why not," Alabaster said. "Seems they were earwigging on our conversation earlier. Maybe I should just come out and tell them everything."

"But Geoffrey isn't here," Gráinne said. "And this is a family matter."

Alabaster shrugged. "This needs to be said. You might wanna be sittin' down."

Aoife and Killian looked like they might vomit. Gráinne looked confused.

Even Seamus didn't look as composed as he'd sounded about not wanting his uncle's money.

"I'm leaving," Alabaster said. "Selling me portion of the estate and gettin' out of town."

Gráinne tipped her head back at the ceiling and laughed. Apparently, that hadn't been discussed at their meeting.

"Don't be laughing," Alabaster said. "Tis not a joke."

"Where yeh off to, uncle?" Aoife asked.

"None of your damn business," Alabaster said.

"This is a bunch of malarkey," Killian said. "We all know you wouldn't make it on your own."

"Who said I'd be alone?" Alabaster asked.

"If you're not taking any of us, who're yeh takin'?" Gráinne asked with a raised eyebrow and a smirk.

"That's neither here nor there." Alabaster waved a hand in the air. "What matters is whether one of yeh want to buy me portion of the estate or not."

Aoife looked like she might pass out.

"I think this would have been a better conversation to have with Geoffrey," Gráinne said. "In private."

I glanced around the room. Every person stared. If small Irish towns were anything like small American ones, the entire population of Ballywick would know about this before the end of the week.

"We both know what he would have said." Alabaster shrugged. "Let me know what you and Donal want to do by tomorrow. Otherwise, it's going on the market." Alabaster nodded once then walked out of the room.

Seamus grabbed my hand almost as if to steady himself.

I had no idea what to say or do to make him feel better.

Gráinne regained her composure first. "Right, well then. I think we need to get the nice bottles of wine from the cellar. I apologize for the airing of our dirty jumpers."

She left the room, and people started to whisper about what had just taken place.

Seamus leaned in and kissed me on the cheek. "I'll go help Mam."

I wanted to hug him. Or at least ask what the implications of all this were, but he was gone before I could.

I'd have plenty of time after everyone went home to talk to him.

"Right before Christmas," Killian said, coming up behind me. "Crazy old man."

I glanced over at him. "Has he threatened this before?"

"Not this specifically." Killian took a sip of his beer, and I did the same. "But it's always something. He throws around his portion of the estate to keep an upper hand over the family."

"Would it be so bad if he sold?"

Killian looked at me like I'd just said I thought England was better than Ireland.

"I'll take that as a yes."

"Removing his portion would render the estate incomplete."

"And is it completely out of the question that one of the families could purchase it?"

Killian shook his head. "It's not that simple." He looked me up and down. "I wouldn't expect a child of a single American mother to understand the complexities of Irish wealth."

I gaped at him as he turned and walked away.

Between Killian's comment and standing at the edge of the crowd, I felt like a complete outsider.

I finished my Guinness and headed toward the kitchen, but it too had people crowded around.

I simply needed a moment to myself.

The bathroom next to the study was open. I quickly ducked inside and locked the door.

My makeup had stayed put exactly as Magella had applied it.

Magella.

I hadn't seen her all evening. She'd said she was going to be at the party, hadn't she?

I'd have to ask Clara after I regained a bit of my composure. Killian obviously didn't like me. But maybe he was simply taking his frustrations with Alabaster out on me.

The bathroom was white with shiny gold flourishes. The door I'd come in wasn't the only one in the room. Another door that probably led to the study was to the right.

I turned on the cold water tap and ran my hands underneath.

When I turned the tap off, I heard a heated exchange coming from the other side of the door.

9

"Alabaster, stop," a woman said. Part of me wondered if I'd traveled back in time and was hearing Alabaster's and Rose's argument again.

I dried my hands, then reached for the handle leading to the study, but it was locked.

"I don't want this, please," the woman pleaded.

I rushed out of the bathroom just as the study door flew open, and Clara came running out, tears streaming down her face.

My feet took me toward the study instead of after Clara.

Alabaster sat at a desk with his back to the door. He had a cell phone to his ear but wasn't speaking.

I stood in the doorway, watching. I probably should have walked away, but my curiosity got the better of me.

"Yes, yes, yes," Alabaster said. "I understand. Just do it. Now."

He ended the call and slammed the phone onto the desk.

His eyes narrowed when he saw me. "Earwigging, are we? Seems all the rage with kids these days."

"What was that with Clara?" I asked, crossing my arms over my chest.

"It's not what you think," he said.

"Really? Because from where I stand, it seems like you enjoy forcing yourself on women." I almost couldn't believe I was confronting him, but I could still feel his tongue trying to part my lips.

I shuddered.

"You don't know what you're talking about," he said. "And if I were you, I'd keep my pretty nose out of it."

"Or what?" I asked. "You've already told Seamus and the entire family that you're disinheriting them, selling the family estate, and moving. What else could you threaten?"

Alabaster didn't stand. "You couldn't possibly understand the complexities—"

"Right," I interrupted. "Because I'm just—as Killian so politely said—the child of a single American mother who knows nothing about Irish wealth."

Alabaster let out a sarcastic laugh. "Like Killian would know anything about Irish wealth. He's a real cute hoor."

"I don't care what Killian said or what he is." I had no idea what a cute hoor was. "But I do care about how you treat women."

"Look, I'm sorry," he said. "I got carried away with the mistletoe. I drank too much, and I shouldn't have tried to kiss you."

"Maybe you should apologize to Clara and Rose, too," I said.

"I need to do a lot more than apologize to Clara," he said. "But right now, I need to take this call."

He picked up his phone and showed me the screen with an incoming call lighting the screen. The contact was Damned Solicitor.

He answered it without my okay. I let myself out of the

room, closing the door behind me slightly louder than was necessary.

I struggled to get control of my emotions. Seamus didn't need his family seeing the over-dramatic Shayla. Heck, he'd barely seen her. I'd figured out in my teen years how to control the drama. Mainly because my mother had insisted.

After a few deep breaths, I calmly headed in the direction Clara had gone.

But after looking for her in all the normal places—the kitchen, the patio, the den—I gave up. I needed some of the wine Gráinne and Seamus had gone to get.

I headed back to the den to find them, but the sound of glass shattering drew my attention back to the study.

I rushed in the other direction, a steady stream of people following behind me.

When I opened the door to the study, my breath caught in my chest.

I turned and faced the people behind me, extending my arms to prevent anyone from coming inside.

"Somebody call the police–er—the Gardaí," I said.

Nobody moved.

I spotted Magella in the crowd. "Magella, could you please call the Gardaí?"

"Why? What's going on?" Her voice was shaky with emotion.

"Just call them and tell them they need to get here as soon as possible with an ambulance," I said.

She hesitated but pulled out her phone.

"As for everyone else, I need you to stay out here, regard-less of what you see," I said. "Do you understand?"

Seamus and Gráinne emerged from a door that probably led to the basement. "What's going on?" Seamus asked.

"Can you stand here, please?" I asked.

He hurried to the front of the crowd and peeked inside. "Is that—"

He'd seen the same thing I had.

"I'm going to check on him," I whispered.

Seamus nodded and turned his back to the study, using his body to block the herd of prying eyes.

Alabaster's feet were the only thing peeking out from around the sofa. The glass that had shattered was all over the carpet from the huge window that looked out toward the front of the house.

A red brick with a blue piece of paper rubber-banded to it was on the floor next to Alabaster. From the looks of it, it hit him in the head. Though whether it had hit him before or after he was on the ground wasn't immediately evident.

I checked for a pulse on the side of Alabaster's neck but found none. Across his closed mouth was some sort of plant . . . mistletoe.

A chill ran down my spine.

This wasn't a freak accident.

This was murder.

10

I did CPR until the ambulance arrived and the medics took over.

"We need to make sure no one leaves the premises before the Gardaí gets here," I said to Seamus. He hurried away in the den's direction.

An official-looking woman walked through the front door. She wore dark pants, a light blue button-down collared shirt, a dark tie, and a dark jacket over top. Her jet-black hair was pulled into a bun at the base of her neck to allow for her hat to perch on top of her head.

"I'm Garda Ryan. Can you tell me what's happened?"

"I was the one who found him initially. When I went into the room, I removed a sprig of what looked like mistletoe from across Alabaster's lips," I said as quietly as I could so no one around us would hear.

Thankfully, it seemed everyone had moved away from the door. "Other than that, I moved nothing. There are a few pillows on the floor that don't belong and a brick that seems to have broken the window. A note is attached with a rubber band, but I couldn't tell if there was a message written on it, and I didn't want to mess with evidence. There was also a cell phone under the desk that looked like it was—"

"Sorry." She held up a hand. "Who are you?"

"Oh, right." Obviously, I should have told her who I was before launching into a crime scene analysis. If someone acted like I had on an investigation I was assigned to, I'd have been taken aback as well.

"I'm Shayla. Seamus' girlfriend from America. I'm a police officer over there."

She frowned. "I heard rumors you'd be here. Just don't go makin' a hames out of things. You Americans think you know more about police work than us silly Irishmen, but I assure you, we can do the job just as well as you, if not better," she mumbled the last part.

Her candor surprised me, but I understood the message. "Of course. I'm sure you have it handled. I was simply trying to relay what I'd seen."

"The only thing you buggered up was the mistletoe, right?"

"I had to remove it to do CPR, but yes, that's all I moved."

She nodded once, then turned back to Alabaster's body.

I took that as my sign to leave.

Before joining everyone in the den, I closed myself into the bathroom and splashed water on my face.

Rylie was the one who knew how to deal with these types of situations. Sure, I was the police officer, but she was the shit magnet. I so badly wanted her to be there with me.

I pulled my phone from my clutch and texted her.

wish you were here. dead body

I sat on the toilet and waited for a reply. It was earlier in

Colorado—evening. She might be eating dinner with her family, but she probably still had her phone.

> What!?!

Her reply came back before I even saw the bubbles that indicated she was typing.

> Who died? Was it murder?

don't know yet. seamus uncle

> Are you investigating?

nope. the gardaí have it under control. basically kicked me out of the room

> Their loss. Oh well. Did he propose yet?

I glanced down at the phone as a lump formed in my throat. Whether it was emotion or exhaustion, the tears formed just the same.

i don't know that he's going to

> He is.

how can you be so sure? did you help him pick out a ring? because when his uncle told him about a family heirloom ring, he said he didn't want it

> I didn't help him pick out a ring. But he's madly in love with you. Why else would he have taken you to Ireland for Christmas?

to meet his family? and because my mom went on that cruise with her boyfriend of the month. he probably just felt sorry for me because I would have been alone for christmas

> You wouldn't have been alone. You would have been with me.

true. but still

> Give him time. He'll pop the question. You just need to know what you'll say.

I considered this for a minute. Of course, I'd say yes. But things had changed so much in less than 24 hours.

When I didn't reply right away, Rylie texted again.

> You are going to say yes, right?

did you know seamus is rich? like ireland's most eligible bachelor who ran away from home to get away from taking over the family business

The text bubbles started, then stopped, then started again. Finally, she replied.

> WHAT!?!

yeah. not that that changes anything, right? or does it

> Why didn't he tell you this before you got there? Did he think you wouldn't notice his castle?

his parents don't own the castle, his aunt and uncle do

I was joking about the castle. But that is HELLA cool. Is it the uncle who just died?

different one

Voices grew louder on the other side of the door leading to the study where the Gardaí were processing Alabaster's body.

gotta go. miss you. wish you were here

Me too. But not because there's a dead body. I'm done with that stuff, remember?

I could feel my eyes roll back in my head, something my mother would have promptly corrected.

yeah. sure

I slipped my phone back into my clutch and tiptoed to the door. I shouldn't have tried to listen, but I couldn't help myself.

"It was the brick," one of the voices said. "It obviously hit him and made him fall."

"The mistletoe was in his mouth," another voice said. "It could have been poisoning. Mistletoe is poisonous, right?"

Had I said it was in his mouth? It hadn't been in his mouth. It had been across his closed lips.

"But it would have taken time to poison him. He would have had to eat it."

"Maybe someone used a pillow to suffocate him," a third voice said.

"Maybe we should stop speculating and let forensics do their jobs."

The chatter stopped. I leaned against the door lever, expecting it to be locked, but in one swift motion, it moved, and the door flew open.

If it wasn't bad enough that Garda Ryan caught me spying on their conversation, I lost my balance, fell forward into the room, and smashed my head on the corner massive wooden desk.

I didn't know whether my head or my ego was more bruised.

"Listening in on our conversation, are yeh?" Garda Ryan said. "Don't think we can solve the case on our own?"

"I-I wasn't." I tried to get to my feet, but my head spun, sending me crashing back to the ground. "I was using the bathroom and fell."

She didn't help me up. "Can someone get her a towel, so she doesn't bleed all over the crime scene?"

I reached up and touched my forehead, my hand coming back covered in red. Head wounds always bled more than other wounds, but the sight of blood made me queasy.

I tried to change my focus. My gaze darted around the room and landed on the cell phone. That was still lit up as if someone was still on the other line.

"You should—"

"Do not tell me what I should do," Garda Ryan said, cutting me off.

"But the—"

"No," she said. "No buts. I told you to stay out of it, and only ten minutes later, I find ya poking your nose into it."

Another Garda handed me a towel—a white towel—for me to press against my head.

I had no choice. I'd either have to ruin Gráinne's towel or bleed all over the crime scene. I pressed the towel to my head just as Seamus walked into the room.

He looked from Garda Ryan to me, then back again.

"Did you sock her, Molly?" Seamus rushed to my side, helping me hold the towel to my head.

"Course I didn't sock her," Molly—aka Garda Ryan—said. "Why would I do a thing like that?"

Seamus eyed her, then returned his attention to me. "Are you okay? I can get the paramedics to come back."

"I'll be fine," I said, not sure if that was true or not. "Just a little bump."

"Yer girlfriend was spying on me investigation," Molly said.

"Me girlfriend is a cop," Seamus said. "She has every right to be part of the investigation."

Molly crossed her arms over her chest. "That so?"

He was not helping the situation. I could almost feel her turning more and more against me.

"It's okay," I said, trying to stand again. Seamus helped me into an upright position. "I wasn't spying, I promise. I don't want to be part of the investigation. But you should know about the phone under the desk."

"Yeh already told me about it," Molly said. "I'll get to it when I get to it."

"Thing is," I said. "It looks like it's still an open line. Someone might have been spying for real."

At that moment, the phone call ended, and the screen went black.

11

Seamus, Molly, and I stood staring at the dark screen.

"Aren't you gonna see who it was?" Seamus asked.

"We're not touching it," Molly said. "It's a piece of evidence. Maybe a key piece."

Seamus sighed heavily. "Look, I know yer probably still angry with me, but can yeh pull the stick out your arse for just a minute to tell us what the hell happened to me uncle?"

She narrowed her dark eyes at Seamus. "Why in the world would I be angry with you? Hmm. Maybe because you took me to America, proposed, then changed your mind. Nah, it must be something else."

"I didn't ask why yeh was angry with me," Seamus said, glancing at me. "I asked what happened to me uncle."

I tried not to react. This was the woman he'd proposed to in America? She was from Ireland?

Both of his ex-fiancées were in this house. My head spun. I felt unsteady on my heels even though Seamus had a tight grip on me.

"He died," she said, her voice completely void of emotion.

The other Garda officers stood around, trying to act like they had heard nothing she said. "And I'll be talking to the both of yeh along with the rest of the guests in the den when I get finished in here."

Seamus shook his head, then turned to me. "Are yeh okay to walk, or do yeh need me to carry ya?"

Molly turned away from us and back to her colleagues, who jolted back into action.

"I can walk," I said.

We left the room through the main door when a thought crossed my mind.

"What's wrong?" Seamus asked when I stopped walking.

I turned back to Molly. "Check the door handle to the bathroom for prints," I said. "Earlier, the door was locked, so you couldn't come in through the bathroom. Now, it's unlocked. I'd guess whoever did this escaped through the bathroom and into the hall."

Molly didn't look thrilled I was still trying to help, but I didn't want her to miss anything. Not that I thought I was better than her or that she couldn't figure it out on her own.

She finally nodded once before crouching down next to Alabaster's body.

"She really should let you help," Seamus said when we were out of earshot. "You're so intuitive about these things."

"I'm sure she has it handled," I said.

He helped me onto one of the couches in the den.

"Oh my goodness, what happened to you?" Gráinne asked, rushing to my side.

"I'm so sorry about your towel," I said. "I'll pay you for it."

"Nonsense," Gráinne said. "It's just a towel. Plus, Magella is brilliant at getting stains out of clothes."

I glanced over at Magella, who held a sobbing Clara, as Edward looked at his wife and mother-in-law helplessly.

Could Clara have killed Alabaster? She seemed a likely suspect after he attacked her.

"Can I get you a drink?" Gráinne asked. "Or an ice pack?"

"Maybe both?" I removed the towel. "How bad is it?"

Seamus looked closer while Gráinne stood.

"Not too bad," he said. "I don't think it'll scar. Quite the bleeder, though."

"Head wounds," I said, smiling at him.

He kissed my cheek. "I'll go fetch something to get the blood off."

The minute he stood, a disheveled and very drunk Aoife plopped down next to me. "If anyone asks, we were together all night."

Was she trying to get me to be her alibi? I gaped at her. "Did you kill Alabaster?"

She tipped her head back and laughed.

I waited for her to finish.

"Oh, yer serious?" She shook her head and lowered her voice. "I was with me boyfriend in the garden. The family doesn't approve." She smoothed down her hair and pulled out what looked like a twig. "Hold on, did something really happen to Uncle Alabaster?"

"I'm sorry," I said. "This probably wasn't the kindest way to tell you. Alabaster died."

Tears welled in her eyes. "But—no—how?"

"Don't know," I said. "The Gardaí are looking into it."

"The guards are here?" She turned and glanced over her shoulder. "Molly too?"

"Yep," Seamus said, handing me a wet towel. "Molly too."

"That sucks," Aoife said without explaining more.

I so badly wanted to take Seamus to the side and tell him to give me a more detailed rundown of his life. I thought we'd practically told each other everything. Not that I had much to tell other than I had a thing for Luke a long time ago. But just because my life didn't consist of fortune, fame, and exes up the wazoo didn't mean he should have kept all this from me.

"Here's your wine and ice," Gráinne said, handing them to me. "You look so much better without all that blood on your face. You can barely see where you were bleeding."

I smiled. It also meant all the makeup Magella applied was now gone. Oh well.

"Thank you all for waiting so patiently," Molly said, marching into the room as if she owned the place. "My colleagues and I will be conducting interviews just as quickly as we can to get you out of here as soon as possible."

A few people groaned while others nodded.

"Can you tell me what happened to my brother?" Gráinne asked, her voice hard and her arms crossed over her chest. Something told me she didn't like any of Seamus' exes.

And that it was best to stay on her good side.

"We're still figuring that out," Molly said. "Would you like me to start with you?"

"Certainly not," Gráinne said. "I'd much prefer speaking with one of your colleagues. And, please, interview the guests first as they may need to be getting home to their loved ones."

Molly looked only slightly deterred by Gráinne's cold shoulder. "Is anyone in dire need of getting out of here tonight?"

No one said anything.

"Anyone particularly excited to be interviewed?" Molly tried for humor, but it landed on deaf ears. "Grand. Then, we'll start with you."

She pointed at Edward. "Please, come with me."

Edward followed, and soon enough, people were going back one by one with different Garda officers.

Clara had regained her composure before she walked back

with Molly. Would she tell Molly about what had happened between her and Alabaster?

When it was Aoife's turn, she winked at me, then turned to Molly and practically shouted, "I don't know why we all have to be interviewed. I was with Shayla when this all happened."

I did my best not to let my jaw hang open. Now if I told the truth, we'd both look suspicious.

I sucked in a breath and tried to decide what to do.

Seamus and his mother were whispering to themselves. I wanted to tell Seamus and see what he thought, but before I could, one of the officers—not Molly—was calling him back.

I couldn't very well ask Gráinne about it since she was probably part of the family who wasn't particularly keen on Aoife's boyfriend. And Aoife had been so nice to me. I never thought I'd have a friend like her. Sure, Rylie was super cool. But Aoife was sparkly and popular and amazing.

My chest constricted. If they didn't approve of Aoife's boyfriend, why would they approve of me? Compared to Nuala, Molly, Aoife, and Clara, I was plain. Boring. Poor. The daughter of a single American mother. Seamus might love me, but would his family? Or were they just being nice to me because Seamus hadn't been home in so long?

12

M olly stood in the doorway, calling my name.

Part of me wanted to ask for someone else to interview me. It was probably against some protocol or something to interview your ex-fiancé's current girlfriend, wasn't it?

Maybe not since she seemed to be heading up her ex-fiancé's uncle's murder investigation.

I stood and did my best to look confident as I followed her out the door.

Other than Gráinne, I was the last to be interviewed.

"Please sit down," she said when we got to the kitchen. "I think we got off on the wrong foot. I'm Molly Ryan."

"Shayla Murphy." I sat across the small round table from her. "Nice to meet you."

"I understand you're a police officer in the United States, so you will likely have ideas about the case that perhaps others would not. However, I'd like you to keep your story as focused on facts as possible. I like to work through my gut reactions before I have anyone else's muddling mine up."

That was understandable. I nodded.

"Can you tell me everything you remember?"

"Starting when?"

"How about since you arrived in Ireland?"

I took a deep breath and told her everything that had happened in the last twenty-four hours in as much factual detail as I could.

When I got to the part about Clara being in the room with Alabaster, she stopped me.

"Do you have a habit of spying on people?"

Her change of tone took me aback. What happened to starting over?

"No," I said. "I was in the bathroom and heard shouts."

"After you'd heard him in a tussle earlier in the evening?"

I shrugged. "Wrong place, wrong time?"

She sat back in her chair. "Continue."

Now I didn't want to tell her anything. I wanted to keep everything to myself.

"I heard Clara and Alabaster arguing. I couldn't make out the words other than I think she said something like—let me go—then stormed out of the study. I went in and spoke with Alabaster, telling him he shouldn't be forcing himself on women."

"And did anyone else hear or see him try these things with the other women?" Molly asked. "Or are we just supposed to take your word for it? Maybe you were mad he tried to kiss you, so you're making him out to be a wanker, so we don't suspect you."

"I was with Aoife when he was killed." The lie slipped out so suddenly, I almost didn't believe I'd said it at all.

She looked down at her tablet. "That's what Aoife said too."

"And as far as anyone else hearing or seeing, I don't know. But I'm not making it up. Everyone saw him try to kiss me.

From what I've heard, he has a bit of a reputation with things like this. Especially when he drinks."

She stared at me for a while, then continued with her questioning. "So you talked to Alabaster, then met up with Aoife. Then what?"

"Then I heard the glass shatter," I said. "I rushed in and found Alabaster lying on the floor dead with mistletoe on top of his mouth, pillows all over the floor, and a brick with a note tied to it next to his head."

"Didn't Alabaster try to kiss you under the mistletoe?" Molly asked, not looking up from the tablet.

"He did," I said.

"And why didn't you let him?"

Was she actually asking me that? "I didn't really want his tongue in my mouth if that's what you're asking."

"And you pushed him hard enough to make him fall?"

"It was an instinct," I said.

"Right," she said. "I suppose they do teach American police officers to hurt others at the slightest inclination of their own perceived danger."

I wanted to stand up and walk out of the room. How dare she insult my profession? Weren't we on the same team? "What do they teach you here? To simply let people assault you for the better good?"

She narrowed her eyes at me. "Is there anything else you'd like to tell me about what happened tonight? Anything you'd like to clarify or change?"

Now was my chance. I could tell her I wasn't really with Aoife. But she'd think I was the one who killed Alabaster. No one had seen me between the time I'd gone to the bathroom and when I'd heard the crash. I had no other alibi.

"No, that's all," I said.

13

I t felt like ages before Seamus and I were finally snuggled up in bed.

"Tomorrow will be better," he said, brushing the hair from my face gently so as not to hurt the bandage on my forehead.

"I don't know how it could be much worse," I said. "I'm so sorry about your uncle."

"He was a nasty old man," Seamus said. "I'm sorry he kissed you."

"I think Molly thinks I killed him," I said.

"Molly's just peeved at me," he said. "Before yeh ask, how about I just tell you the story?"

"That would be great."

"I met Molly just after Nuala and I broke up," he said. "She was new to town and ended up being a rebound to top all rebounds. She convinced me we didn't need my family or Ireland. Told me she wanted to start fresh with me. In America. I thought I was in love. We left without telling me mam and da. Only told Killian, actually."

Killian? Where had he been all night? I'd hardly seen him

after his failed proposal when he'd charged after his uncle. He'd definitely be a suspect.

"But when we got to the States, and she realized I'd left me money in Ireland, she turned heel and ran."

That was not what I'd been expecting. "But I thought you proposed in the States?"

"That I did," he said. "With a ring I could afford on me summie salary. At first, she pretended to like it, but when I told her she'd have to get a job to help pay the rent, that sent her through the roof. Dodged a bullet with that one."

"I guess I should thank her then," I said. "For leaving you alone so we could meet."

He pulled me closer to him and kissed me. "It's so nice to be able to trust someone."

My insides twisted. I hadn't actually lied to him, but I'd lied nonetheless. "I need to tell you something."

He flinched back as if I'd burned him. "What is it?" His tone of voice was afraid. "Please don't tell me yer breaking up with me."

"Oh no, nothing like that," I said.

He relaxed slightly.

"It's about my alibi." I shifted onto my side to face him. "I wasn't with Aoife when Alabaster was killed. I wasn't with anyone. I was looking for Clara."

"Why would yeh be looking for Clara?"

"Because Alabaster was in his study with her, and it sounded like he was attacking her," I said. "She ran out, and I confronted Alabaster, but then I went to find Clara."

"Then why'd yeh say you were with Aoife?" He settled back down and put his arm around me again.

"It was initially her idea, something about being with a guy the family doesn't like?"

He groaned. "Chadwick?"

"I've no idea," I said. "She didn't tell me his name, only that the family doesn't approve."

My stomach twisted with the thought of his family, potentially not approving of me, either. "Why don't they approve?"

"He's rough with her," Seamus said. "From what Killian said, he's left bruises on her in the past. She swears he's changed, but no one is convinced."

That made sense.

"When she first asked me to say we were together, I wasn't going to do it. I was going to tell the truth. But then Molly started acting like she thought I did it. And, well, it just slipped out of my mouth before I could stop it."

Seamus considered me for a minute before he burst out laughing.

I chuckled. "What?"

"I don't care if you lied about your alibi," he said. "It's probably best you did, seeing as how Molly's still a wee bit pissed about what happened with us."

"Do you think she'll want you back?" I asked.

Seamus kissed my neck. "Doesn't matter what she wants. I have everything I want right here."

"What if she finds out I lied?" I asked. "Do you think she'll send me to jail?"

"Probably," he said.

My stomach felt like it did a flip-flop. "Probably?"

Seamus shrugged. "We just can't let her find out. And in the meantime, I think we should look into the murder ourselves, just to be safe."

"To be safe?" I asked. "Do you think someone else might be in danger?"

"Yeah," he said. "You."

"Me? You think whoever hurt Alabaster might hurt me?"

"Nothing like that," he said. "But if we can figure out who

murdered him, then you'll definitely be off the hook for not having an alibi, right?"

It made sense. "But Molly told me to stay out of it. I'd want someone to respect me if I asked them to stay out of one of my cases."

"Rylie pokes her nose in all the time."

"Rylie's different," I said.

"How? She's not a police officer? She has no formal training? She has no business investigating anything more than a fishing violation?"

"That may be true—all of it—but Rylie's special. She has a way of figuring things out."

"And you don't think you do?"

"I don't know," I said. "I never guessed you were so wealthy. Never."

"That's because I'm not wealthy," Seamus said. "Me mam and da are."

"You know what I mean."

He lifted my chin so our gazes met. His eyes sparkled in the moonlight, peeking through the sheer curtains. "You need to give yourself more credit. Tomorrow, we'll start poking around. What's the worst that could happen?"

14

The worst that could happen? Well, end up in prison. Or die.

I hadn't spoken these thoughts aloud in bed when Seamus asked. I'd simply smiled and let him kiss me.

But the next morning, over coffee and a plate full of meat —the traditional Irish breakfast, I was told—I almost voiced my concerns.

I didn't have a chance, though, because Aoife waltzed into the kitchen just as I was opening my mouth. She had on thigh-high baby blue suede boots, a super short ruffled skirt, and a long-sleeved t-shirt with the name of a designer on it.

"You naughty girl," Seamus said to her. "I'm going to tell yer mam and da that you were with Chadwick last night."

Her eyes widened. She looked at me. "You told him?"

"I don't like to keep secrets from him," I said. "But I told the police we were together."

She didn't look appeased by this. "I don't care about the police. I care about me family. They'll cut me off."

"Don't think you'll be losing much there," Seamus said.

"What's that supposed to mean?" Aoife asked.

Seamus looked at her the same way he looked at me when I didn't understand the punchline of a joke. "Come on. You have to know."

"Know what?" Aoife looked utterly unaware of whatever he was trying to tell her.

"Your family is broke. That's why yer parents weren't here last night—they were trying to find a buyer for the castle."

Aoife gasped. "They're selling the castle?"

"Have to," Seamus said. "Yer da's gone into too much debt."

"But what about Uncle Alabaster? Now that he's gone won't the money transfer to our families? To us? I'll buy the castle."

"Uncle Alabaster changed his will," Seamus said. "Probably cut all of us out."

"No." Aoife shook her head. "He didn't. I saw the will less than a week ago. The solicitor's out of town for the entire month."

Who left their will out for their nieces and nephews to see? I didn't have much experience with all that, but I always thought rich people liked to keep their finances secret.

"He was working with someone else in the office," Seamus said. "That's why they were all fighting yesterday and why he didn't give Killian the ring."

She put her fists on her hips and cocked her head to one side. "If he's not giving us the money, who is he giving it to?"

Seamus shrugged. "Beats me. But I'd assume we'll find out when the solicitor comes back to town."

"What about the person in the office?" Aoife asked. "The one Uncle was working with?"

"I guess they don't have the authority to discuss the will with the family in the event of a death." Seamus took a bite of his breakfast, then promptly spat it back out. "Did Magella make this?"

No one could answer his question. Only Aoife and I were in the kitchen with him. But the breakfast didn't taste as awful to me as he was insinuating.

"I think Alabaster was on the phone with the solicitor last night," I said.

Both Aoife and Seamus turned to look at me.

"What makes you think that?" Seamus asked.

"When I confronted him after his run-in with Clara, he held the phone up and showed me the person calling him. It was Damned Solicitor."

"Sounds about right," Seamus said with a laugh.

"I can't believe they're selling the castle," Aoife said. "I had plans. They knew I had plans."

That was probably why they hadn't told her. I couldn't imagine having to let your child down like that.

"Have you been that out of touch that you didn't see what was going on right under your nose?" Seamus asked. "I've been out of the country, and even I knew."

"I've been busy."

"With a boyfriend who treats you like trash, a social media profile that makes you look like a hooker, and enough clothes for the entire population of Ireland." Seamus was never one to hold back.

"Maybe I could sell my clothes," Aoife said. "Maybe then we could keep the castle."

Seamus didn't reply. Her clothes probably wouldn't pay for an entire castle, but I wasn't very knowledgeable about how much clothes cost. Or castles.

"I'm happy to be your alibi," I said, reaching over and laying a hand on Aoife's arm, "but stay away from that guy. I know you can find another one who treats you right."

It was then that I noticed a bruise on her wrist. When she caught me staring, she pulled her sleeve down to cover it, then glanced at Seamus to find out if he'd seen it too.

He was still analyzing his breakfast—taking bites and spitting them out in disgust.

"Seriously," I said, my voice lowered. "You do not need to be with someone who hurts you."

She bent over and hugged me tightly. "You're right. I'll break it off with him."

"Good." I patted her on the back.

"Do you like breakfast?" Gráinne asked, coming into the kitchen wearing a dirty apron and a chef's hat.

Seamus didn't turn around to look at her before he said, "It's terrible. Did Magella quit?"

Gráinne's face drooped.

When she didn't reply, he turned then said, "Damn. I'm sorry, Mam. I didn't mean I don't like it. It's just different. I'll get used to it."

She smiled, though her eyes glistened with tears. "Magella had to tend to some family matters with Clara, so I thought I'd try my hand at breakfast. I'm sorry it was terrible. I should have known I'd be no good in the kitchen."

Seamus stood and wrapped an arm around her shoulders. "You may be terrible in the kitchen, but the way you are with the horses and the business is beyond anything I've ever seen. We can't all be good at everything."

"What mother isn't good at cooking?" Gráinne asked.

"Where does it say a mother has to be good at cooking?" Seamus said. "You're the best mam I could have ever asked for."

Tension settled in the room that I suspected came from the question of, if she was such a good mother, why hadn't he been home in so long? But the question remained unspoken.

"Did you know me parents are selling the castle?" Aoife asked.

"I did," Gráinne said.

"Why didn't ya tell me?"

"I thought yeh knew. Geoffrey said he talked to you about it." Gráinne turned her attention from Aoife to me, giving me an apologetic look. "I'm sorry for all the drama since you've been here. This happens every time we have company."

"Company?" Aoife laughed. "Shayla here's basically family, isn't she, Seamus?"

Seamus stood staring at her for what felt like a solid minute.

"Either way," Gráinne said when the silence became so awkward, I was about to excuse myself. "The castle is being sold. Alabaster is dead. And life as we've known it will be forever changed."

15

Once Seamus had choked down some breakfast along with a large amount of coffee, he took me on a tour of the property.

The house was even bigger than it looked from the outside with a massive basement including a pool and movie theater. Everything was decorated in a cozy, chic manner, with various touches here and there referencing the equestrian nature of the property and Christmas lights tastefully placed.

The garden was covered in a thin layer of snow that must have come overnight.

"Usually, this entire area is covered with flowers," Seamus said. He held my gloved hand in his as we made our way to the nearest pasture, where a few horses galloped around. "The horses can be finicky, so no need to feel bad if they don't take to you."

But he didn't need to worry. Every single horse I came to let me rub their nose. Even the ones who wouldn't let Seamus.

"Yer a natural," Seamus said, his gaze trained on me as I stroked the soft neck of a tall black horse.

"They're lovely creatures," I said. "I always wanted a horse growing up. One year for my birthday, my mom told me we would go horseback riding in the mountains. But she got called away on a case, and I had to celebrate with the neighbors. That's as close as I've ever been to riding a horse."

"Would you like to ride?" Seamus asked.

I whipped around to face him. "Could I? I thought these were racehorses?"

"These are," he said. "And my mother would murder us both if we rode them. But we have other horses too. Casual riding horses."

My heart felt like it might beat out of my chest. "I'd love to. When? Where? How? I didn't bring any boots or anything."

"That reminds me," Seamus said. "Mam asked if she could take you shopping in town this afternoon. I'd like to catch up with a few friends, but we could meet back up for dinner?"

Nervousness replaced the excitement. "I didn't bring a lot of money. Only enough to buy some Christmas gifts for your family and—"

"Mam's already insisted she pay for everything," he said. "Don't even try to pull out your money at the registers."

"If Alabaster cut you all out of the will and Aoife's parents are broke, are your parents going to be okay?"

"My parents?" Seamus asked.

"I'm sorry if that's too personal a question," I said, quickly realizing it probably was. But I wasn't the one who was discussing the family finances in front of—well—me.

"No, not at all," Seamus said.

"And I don't ask because I care about the money. I don't,"

I added. "I just don't want your family to struggle because of taking me shopping."

He squeezed my hand. "My parents are very good with their money. In fact, I suspect if they wanted to buy Uncle Alabaster's place and Uncle Geoffrey's, they could."

"But they don't want to? Hasn't it been in the family for a long time?"

"They don't want to bail Uncle Geoffrey out again," he said. "Aoife doesn't know, but my parents have basically paid for her entire adult life."

"What about Killian?" I asked.

"He'd kill me if he knew I was telling you this." Seamus ran a hand through his hair.

"Then don't," I said. "It's really none of my business."

"It's all right. Killian has been supporting his parents—bailing them out of trouble just as much as me parents have. When he found out the bank was foreclosing on the castle after he thought he'd been paying the mortgage, he moved out and cut them off completely."

"Wow. So what will happen to your Uncle Geoffrey and your Aunt Shannon?"

"Mam and Da agreed to let them live in the guesthouse. The smaller building next to the big house."

"And they're okay with that?"

"Not even a wee bit." Seamus laughed. "But they have no choice. Even if they sell it, they'll hardly be able to pay their other creditors. Without Mam and Da, they'd be going to jail. The guesthouse is slightly better than jail."

I would guess it was more than slightly better.

"Either way, Aoife will be fine. She'll still have all her expensive clothes and shoes and fancy cars." He laughed.

"But not the castle. Not her dream."

He shrugged.

"Do you ever get jealous that your parents pay for Aoife's life but not yours?" I asked.

Seamus laughed again. Harder this time. "Mam and Da would give me every last dollar they had if I wanted it. I made it clear to them I wanted to make my own way in America. And they've respected that."

I tucked myself under his arm and squeezed him around the waist. "That's very impressive of you."

He hooked a finger under my chin and tilted my face up so our lips could meet in a gentle kiss.

"I love yeh, Shayla," Seamus said.

"I love you too."

16

A shiny black car picked Gráinne and me up after I'd gotten myself together for shopping. I wore my best pair of dark skinny jeans, white tennis shoes, a pink blouse, and a jacket. Gráinne wore something similar —only she looked more like she was about to step onto a prized show horse with her attire.

"Seamus tells me you'd like to learn to ride," she said as the driver turned out of the massive driveway onto the wrong side of the road.

Or at least wrong from my experience. Who was I to say it was wrong? It was right to them. Not that there was a right or wrong about which side of the road you drove on. It was morally neutral.

"Shayla?" Gráinne asked.

Shoot.

I'd lost myself in my thoughts.

"Yes, I'd like that very much. If it's okay?"

"It's more than okay," she said, her face lighting up. "It's wonderful. Aoife and Shannon have no interest in the horses, and all the boys' girlfriends have been more interested in how much they were worth than what they could do."

"That must have been so hard," I said. "I can't imagine Seamus dealing with that."

"I can imagine it well," Gráinne said. "Donal and I were much like you and Seamus. He grew up an only child of a single mam. He and I met when I was away from the wealth, on a humanitarian trip. He was completely taken aback when he found out I had money. In fact, he almost left me because of it."

"I can understand that," I said.

Her eyes widened, and she shifted in the seat to face me. "Please tell me you're not thinking of leaving Seamus. It's not his fault his family is wealthy. We have no preconceived notion he'll follow in our footsteps—though I'd love for him to—but if he wants to make his way in America with you, we're all for it."

I smiled at her. "I'm not planning on leaving him. I can just understand how Donal might have felt. Less than, unworthy, completely out of his depth."

She reached over and took my hand in hers. "You are not less than. Not unworthy. And you're not out of your depth. Money is not an indication of someone's value. If it takes money to make you who you are, you shouldn't have it in the first place."

"Thank you," I said, trying not to tear up. "That means a lot to me." I couldn't believe I'd just bared my soul to her like that. It had to have been the hand holding. My mother never held my hand. She was not one for physical affection. Even with her boyfriends. Sometimes, I wondered how she created me at all.

"Now—" She righted herself in her seat. "—let's set some ground rules for this excursion."

I nodded. I was glad she was going to give me a budget. That way, I wouldn't overstep.

"One—you will not pay for anything yourself."

Seamus had already given me that rule, but I still had to ask, "Are you certain?"

"Absolutely," she said. "Two—there is no spending limit, and we will not be looking at price tags. The shops know my limits and will keep us within them. If they show you something, it's within my limit. Understood?"

No spending limit? I wanted to pinch myself to make sure this wasn't a dream.

"Understood?" she repeated.

I nodded.

"Three—you must try on everything I send you into the dressing room with. However, do not feel obligated to get anything simply because I like it. I have an eye for what clothing works on people, but I don't expect you to like everything I do. Please, if you won't wear it or will feel uncomfortable in it, do not get it simply to please me."

That was a fair rule.

"And four—the most important rule of them all—you must have fun. If we end up doing something that isn't fun, tell me right away, and we will change courses. If you tire of trying things on—even after one or two items—that's fine, just tell me. I expect you to be completely honest with me, and I will return the favor. There is no room for dishonesty when it comes to family or shopping."

My insides twisted. "I wasn't with Aoife last night when Alabaster was killed."

She waved a hand as if to shoo the thought away. "I heard you talking this morning in the kitchen. Aoife is a terrible judge of character when it comes to men. I applaud you for trying to cover for her. And for being honest with me. Is there anything else you need to tell me?"

I thought about it for a minute. "Nope. I think that's it."

"Good," she said, seemingly pleased with my answer. "Now, where would you like to begin?"

Ballywick was packed with high-end clothing boutiques, artisanal coffee shops, a couple of old castle-looking churches, and a traditional pub right at the end of town.

We started on one side of the street, making our way toward the pub. The weather was sunny but chilly, the snow from the previous night still hanging out in the shady spots of the sidewalk.

The first shop we went inside smelled of cinnamon and vanilla. A man, probably in his mid-thirties, met us at the door.

"Gráinne, it's been too long," he said, his voice high-pitched, as rushed to us. "What can I do for you? Is this the lovely Shayla I've heard so much about?"

How had he heard about me? I glanced at Gráinne, but she seemed just as confused as I was.

"You've heard about Shayla?" she asked, her tone protective.

"Oh dear, have you not seen the papers?" He hurried back to the counter and pulled a newspaper out to show us.

The headline read: Shayla Murphy—Gold Digger

I gasped.

Gráinne tore the paper from his hands. "This is terrible. To accuse Shayla of being after Seamus' money is downright despicable."

"It wouldn't be the first time he found a mot who was only interested in his money," the man said, giving me a once over.

"It's been nice seeing you, but I think we'll take our business elsewhere." Gráinne turned and walked toward the door, still clutching the crumpled paper in her hands.

The man tried to object, but Gráinne acted as if she didn't hear him.

Once we were outside and the door was closed, she plunged the paper into the nearest garbage can, then turned to me. "You must not listen to anyone who wants to criticize you. Seamus knows who you are. His da and I know who you are. And you know who you are. That's all that matters in this situation."

I smiled. "I can't believe I almost had to use rule four so quickly in our day."

She smiled back.

"It's okay," I said. "I can handle a bit of speculation. Honestly, they don't know me. It's only natural they'd think I'd be after the money. Especially with his history. But what's a mot?"

Gráinne laughed. "It means girlfriend."

"Ah, that makes sense."

"Onto the next shop?"

"Onto the next shop." I nodded once.

The moment we walked through the glass doors of the next boutique, Gráinne announced, "If I hear one word spoken against Shayla's character, we will leave without making a single purchase."

The three employees looked at her with wide eyes.

"Do I make myself clear?" Gráinne asked.

They nodded vigorously.

"Grand," Gráinne said. "Now, we're going to need to start with some riding attire."

The three women practically fell over themselves to help us.

One retrieved us glasses of champagne, another took our

jackets and ushered us to couches outside the dressing rooms, and the third brought the clothes.

All the clothes.

Jeans that made mine look like they'd come from a big box chain store. Boots that probably cost over six months' wages. Dresses and heels and blouses and jackets.

Every piece went through Gráinne first, then to me. She was right—she had an eye for fashion.

I tried everything on as she'd instructed.

Most I liked. Some I didn't. But some surprised me. Things I would never have looked at twice on my own made me look the best.

My favorite was an asymmetrical green dress that Gráinne insisted I wear for the Christmas party.

Gráinne sent me away while she paid, but I'm almost certain I overheard one of the saleswomen say, "It'll be a very happy Christmas for the three of us this year."

I couldn't believe how wonderful it felt to be doted on by Gráinne. Then guilt settled into my gut. What would my mother think if she knew I was here bonding with another mother figure? She might not have been the most loving mom, but she'd always taken care of me. Made sure I was safe. Bought me what I needed at her own expense.

"Is everything okay?" Gráinne asked. "Are yeh knackered?"

I shook my head and plastered a smile back on my face. "Nope. I was just lost in thought."

"Would you fancy a pint before we head down the other side of the street?"

My head was already buzzing from the champagne, but it sounded like a good chance to spend some more time with Gráinne.

I pushed the guilt away.

If my mother wanted to be with me for Christmas, all she would have had to do was say so.

17

The pub was the exact opposite of the boutique. Where the boutique had been bright and open, the pub was dark with big wooden booths and a long bar lined with heavy-looking stools.

Gráinne and I took a booth in the very center. "You can hear all the gossip from this booth. Acoustics and all."

She gave me a sly smile.

I laughed. "That's good to know."

"Ireland—especially the small towns—are all about the scuttlebutt."

"What's the craic, Gráinne?" the barkeep—a man probably in his late seventies with a bald head and a round physique—asked.

"Divil a bit. A couple o'pints for us," she said. "The black stuff."

"A round of Guinness coming up," he said before walking away with a pronounced limp.

"That's Harry. His family's been friends of our family for ages. If there's one person you don't want to mess with in an Irish town, it's the local pub owner."

"Why's that?" I asked.

"'Cause the pub is where everything happens in an Irish town. Round about six or seven, the musicians will start pouring in along with the customers. If yer lucky, you'll make it out by morning." She glanced around. "And if you make the owner mad, he won't let you in, which is practically like being socially banished."

Harry came back with a couple of glasses filled with a dark liquid that almost looked like a mix between thick chocolate milk and root beer. Gráinne ordered a basket of fish and chips while I went with the Guinness pie.

"That's strange," Gráinne said when Harry had gone. "Harry didn't mention me brother."

"Maybe he hasn't heard?"

"Oh, I assure you, everyone's heard," she said. "I suspect it's because they've never really seen eye to eye. I suppose he hasn't really seen eye to eye with either of my brothers, but that's mostly because Geoffrey owes him money. Though, Geoffrey owes many people money."

Two women walked through the doors and hurried over to our booth, stopping the conversation in its tracks.

"I'm so sorry about Alabaster," the taller one said.

Both women were around Gráinne's age and wore jeans with heavy jackets.

"Thank you," Gráinne said.

"I bet you were rather thrilled to see him go, though," the shorter one said with a smirk.

Gráinne glanced at me, then back at her. "Why would you go saying a thing like that?"

"The talk is that he was causing a lot of problems for the family," she said. "Lots of folks are sayin' it was an inside job."

I could feel my jaw drop open.

"What are yeh goin' on about?" Gráinne said.

The other two women exchanged knowing looks.

"Go on, say what's on yer minds," Gráinne insisted.

"He was changing the will, isn't that right? Cuttin' the lot of yeh out?" the taller one said.

"And how would you have gotten such information?" Gráinne asked.

"Yeh know how well secrets keep in Ballywick," the short one said. "It's no bother, though. No one's looking at you."

Gráinne kept her composure but said nothing more.

"I suppose we better be sitting down," the tall one said. "Sorry again."

Gráinne smirked at them as they left.

"They think Geoffrey killed Alabaster?" I asked, my voice at a whisper.

"Shhh." She put a finger to her lips. "Listen."

I took a sip of my Guinness and sat forward, listening. Then, as if they were right next to us, the two women's voices wound their way to my ears.

"She obviously did it," the shorter one's voice echoed above me. "Did you see how she didn't even care when you brought it up?"

I almost said something to Gráinne, but she held up a hand.

Right, we were listening.

"I heard her horse business was gettin' shut down, and they were going bankrupt," the taller one said.

"Who told you that?"

"Rose."

"And how would she know?"

"She and Alabaster were getting back together."

Gráinne's eyes narrowed as if she was thinking about this. Then she shook her head at me.

"What happened to his secret lady?"

"No one knows. She was a secret, after all. And if anyone knew how to keep a secret, it was Alabaster O'Malley."

"What are you ladies having other than a nasty chit-chat about Gráinne?" Harry asked.

"Come on, Harry, you know as well as we do she's not everything she portrays," the shorter one said. "You were saying just the other day—"

Harry cleared his throat loudly, then said, "I don't know what you think you heard me say, but I'd never say anything against Gráinne. Alabaster and Geoffrey are different matters, but Gráinne is a gem."

"But—"

"No buts," he interrupted the shorter woman. "Are you here to eat or to gossip?"

"Didn't know we had to choose between the two," the taller woman said.

When Harry didn't laugh, they both ordered a pint and some chips.

I looked at Gráinne to see if we were going to talk now, but she held her finger up, indicating one more second.

"Harry's losing it," the taller woman said. "He probably thought he was talking to someone else the other day. His eyesight's not as sharp as he'd like to make it out to be. He called me by my sister's name just a few weeks ago."

"Well, yeh are twins."

"Fraternal twins. And my hair is much shorter. Speaking of her, did you hear she went off to London with a man she met online?"

Gráinne sat back in the booth, obviously uninterested in the tall woman's twin going to London with some random man.

"Are you okay?" I asked.

"It's nothing new," she said. "When you have money, people always be wanting you to fail."

"It's none of my business, so tell me if you don't want to say, but is the business in trouble?"

She shook her head. "Not in the slightest. They probably mixed up Geoffrey's business and mine. That's all."

Harry brought our food over and set it down as if he'd had no part in the conversation with the other women. "Anything else you need?"

"No, thank you," Gráinne said with a smile.

He nodded and limped away.

"Let's keep the acoustics our little secret, shall we?" Gráinne asked.

18

Gráinne took me back to the house to get ready for dinner.

"Wear the silver one," she said with a wink before heading out to the stables.

Magella was very quiet when she did my hair and makeup.

"Are you sure you're okay?" I asked when I caught her wiping a tear from her eye.

"I'm sorry. This is incredibly unprofessional. I should have just taken the day off."

"No, it's okay," I said quickly. "I'm only concerned. Is Clara okay?"

Magella's gaze shot up to meet mine. "Why would you ask if Clara's okay?"

Shoot.

Clara probably didn't tell anyone that I'd heard Alabaster attacking her minutes before he wound up dead.

"I heard her with Alabaster in the study."

"What exactly did you hear?" Magella asked.

My intuitional tingles went bonkers with that question.

"She sounded distressed. Then she ran out, and I confronted Alabaster until his attorney called."

"You confronted him? About what?" Magella tugged harder on my hair than was necessary to smooth my curls.

"About how he treated Clara and that other woman," I said. "He blew me off, though. I'm just really sorry you have to deal with this."

She considered me for a moment, then finally said, "I don't know what you saw, but it might not have been what you thought. And what other woman are you talking about?"

"Rose," I said. "Nuala's mother."

Her eyes widened. "Rose and Alabaster were alone together?"

"I found them in the study earlier in the evening. It sounded like he was trying to kiss her under the mistletoe, just like he'd tried with me, but she resisted. He said she came onto him, but the women in town seemed to think they might get back together."

She furrowed her brow but kept smoothing my hair.

"What really happened with him and Clara?" I asked.

Magella turned away from me and acted like she was cleaning the hair out of the brush. "That's not my story to tell."

"I'd love to speak to Clara if she's up for it."

"The guards already spoke to her," Magella said. "And I assure you, she's done nothing wrong."

"I wasn't implying anything," I said. "I'm sorry, I didn't mean it like that."

She turned back and looked at me. "No need to apologize. This has simply been a stressful time for all of us."

I thought about that for a moment. It hadn't seemed to be terribly stressful for Gráinne. In fact, Magella seemed to be taking the entire situation harder than Gráinne.

Though Magella was upset because of her daughter,

whereas Gráinne was dealing with the loss of a brother she didn't seem to really like all that much.

"No matter," Magella said. "You look stunning. Seamus will be a fool not to pro—"

A knock at the door interrupted her.

She hurried off to answer it while I sat staring at my reflection.

Had she almost said propose? Is that why Gráinne had insisted I wear the silver dress and had winked at me?

"Are you about ready?" Seamus poked his head in the door. I could almost swear his eyes turned into hearts like those cute little emoji guys Rylie was always comparing my yellow VW Bug to. I loved it when he looked at me like that.

"I think so." I glanced at Magella for her final approval.

She nodded. "You look amazing."

"I second that," Seamus said, stepping into the room, looking rather dashing himself. He wore a dark blue suit with silver cufflinks and a silver tie.

"You don't look bad yourself," I said.

He kissed me gently on the cheek, his lips sending shivers down my neck. "Shall we?"

Magella kissed him on the cheek as he walked by and gave me a quick hug, whispering in my ear, "You look perfect for tonight."

I quirked an eyebrow up at her, and she winked.

I couldn't tell whether everyone was looking at us differently—with bigger smiles—or whether it was just wishful thinking, but even the driver kept looking in the rearview mirror and smiling at us.

Seamus grabbed my hand. "Are you doing okay?"

"I'm great."

"Did you have fun with Mam today?"

"It was wonderful," I said. "She's a lot of fun to be around."

"I hear she had a grand time with you too." He squeezed my hand. "She always wanted a daughter. Aoife is the closest thing she has, and that's not saying much."

"They don't shop together?"

"Aoife wouldn't be caught dead shopping with me mam."

"Are her parents going to be okay after all of this?"

"They'll be fine," he said. "Uncle Geoffrey needs a good swift kick in the fanny. Aunt Shannon too. Living in our guesthouse won't exactly be a poor living, but it might be a wake-up call."

"How'd they lose so much money?"

"Gambling on risky business ventures mostly," Seamus said. "They were always coming up with some new thing that was going to make them rich. I guess no one told them they were already rich."

We laughed at his joke.

"Mam and Da had the business which they've success-fully run for years. Uncle Alabaster hoarded every penny, investing in the most conservative ways possible."

"There were a couple of women at the pub saying some-thing about your mom's business going under," I said. "Do you think that's possible?"

He shook his head. "That's been the scuttlebutt since I was a kid. I used to get teased on the playground about ending up poor in a gutter. I learned to tune it out."

That's what I suspected, but I didn't want to keep it from him.

"Enough about that," he said. "Tonight is about us."

Butterflies swirled in my stomach.

Us.

"Thank you for bringing me here. I've had a great time meeting your family."

"Other than Uncle Alabaster, eh?"

"Can I ask you a question about that?"

"Go ahead."

"Your family doesn't seem to be too broken up about his passing—you included."

"Ah." He ran a hand through his hair. "It's probably a bit of a relief, to be honest with ya."

"How so?"

"He was a nasty old chap. Holding his money above our heads like it mattered. Causing all sorts of trouble around town. If it wasn't one thing, it was another with him. Are we sad? Sure, in our own ways. He was family, after all. But other than that, he was a bit of a thorn in our sides."

"Please tell me you didn't say any of that to the police."

He laughed. "Course I didn't. If you and Rylie have taught me anything, it's when to keep me mouth shut."

I couldn't tell whether the butterflies had simply landed at the bottom of my stomach or if his answer left me unsettled. Either way, I didn't like it.

Seamus reached over and squeezed my hand, giving me a handsome smile. I was worried about nothing. He was the love of my life.

As the twinkle lights of the town came into view, the butterflies took flight once more. This could be the night that changed everything.

19

Sweat beaded across Seamus' forehead. We'd gotten through cocktails, appetizers, dinner, and dessert.

All that was left was the smidgeon of coffee left in our mugs.

Was he going to do it?

Maybe he wasn't.

Maybe I'd gotten every bit of my hopes up for nothing.

This was just a chance to meet his family.

To spend Christmas together.

He'd turned down Alabaster's ring. Said he didn't need one.

Which either meant he already had one, or he really didn't need one.

At all.

I sipped my coffee as Seamus slipped from his seat and knelt next to me.

I nearly choked on the sip I'd taken.

This was it.

"Shayla?" He fumbled for something in his jacket pocket, his gaze scanning the restaurant.

Probably for any random cameras that had made it past the bouncer at the front door.

Did I mention this place was incredibly posh? As in the nicest restaurant I'd ever stepped foot inside?

"Shayla," he said again, still fumbling. Then his gaze landed on something, and he stopped what he was doing and redirected his attention to his shoe. "I think I dropped a cufflink somewhere."

I glanced down. He was missing a cufflink.

"Am I interrupting something?" Molly asked, coming up next to us. She didn't look too terribly upset that she'd possibly just interrupted Seamus' proposal.

But had he been proposing? Or had he truly lost a cufflink?

"I lost a cufflink," Seamus said as if answering my question. "I was just looking for it."

Molly bent down to grab something from the carpet. "This it?"

She dropped it into Seamus' open hand.

"Thanks," he said and stood.

I looked up at the two of them, then stood as well.

"Stay seated," Molly said. "I have a few questions I'd like to ask you."

"Now?" Seamus asked. "You interrupted our date to ask us questions?"

A few people turned to see what was going on.

I wanted to duck under the table and disappear.

Not only had I thought Seamus was proposing, now he was in an argument with his ex-fiancée in the middle of our date.

"This is of an urgent manner," she said. "We've no time to waste."

"Did you determine a cause of death?" I asked.

She glared at me.

"Look," Seamus said. "If you want our help, you have to answer some of our questions too."

Molly glanced around. "Not here. Anyone could be listening."

"I think we were just about finished anyway," Seamus said, a tinge of irritation in his voice. "Can you wait for us outside?"

I didn't want him to propose now. Not like this. Not in a rush after his ex had disturbed everything.

She hesitantly turned and walked out.

Seamus held my seat for me to sit, and, once I had, he sat in his own. Thank goodness he hadn't gone for the ring in his pocket. If there even was a ring in his pocket. Maybe he really had been down there to find a cufflink.

"I'm sorry about the interruption," he said. "But this is good, right? If they're coming to us for help, that means they don't suspect you of committing the murder."

"I didn't commit the murder," I said, my irritation coming out in my tone.

"I know that," he said. "You don't think I think you did it, do you?"

I shook my head. "No."

"Good," he said, handing the server a credit card without even looking at the tab. "I don't know who killed him, but I know it wasn't you."

We sipped our coffee in silence. I couldn't help but imagine how this night could have ended differently.

When we walked outside, we were hit with wave after wave of flashing lights. "Seamus, Shayla, over here," one of the photographers called. "Did you propose?"

Seamus wrapped a protective arm around me and guided me to the car, where the driver held the door open for us.

"Was that Molly Ryan we saw coming out of the restaurant? Is she heading up your uncle's death investigation?"

another photographer asked. "Or are the two of you getting back together?"

Seamus ignored them.

"Come on, just one good photo, so we don't have to publish trash in the morning," the first photographer said with a smirk.

Seamus looked down at me. I shrugged.

We stood as if we were on the red carpet, me holding myself as tall as I could manage the way I'd been instructed my entire life.

Once they got their photos, we slid into the back seat of the car.

"Figured I'd ride along," Molly said, nearly making me fall back out of the car. Thankfully, the driver was still there to lend a helpful hand. He steadied me and closed the door so seamlessly, I was certain the photographers hadn't even caught the gaffe.

At least, I hoped they hadn't.

"Couldn't you ride with your partner?" Seamus asked.

"This is about as private a place as any," Molly said. "Driver, will you please roll up the partition for us?"

The driver nodded at her in the rearview mirror, and the partition between the front of the car and the back glided upwards.

"I need to know if your family has cameras," Molly said, jumping right into the subject at hand.

Seamus nodded. "Course they do."

"Inside or just outside?"

"If you think you'll be able to see what happened from a camera in the study, think again," Seamus said. "There are no cameras in there."

"What about the hallway just outside? Or outside the window?"

I felt practically invisible as they discussed between the

two of them. Seamus was turned to face Molly, his back to me.

I pulled out my phone to a message from Rylie.

"I don't know the specifics," Seamus said. "It's been ages since I've had knowledge of my family's security systems."

Did he propose yet?

"Do you think they'd let me take a peek at the footage?" Molly asked.

"Without a warrant?" Seamus laughed. "Not a chance."

I typed a response.

no. i thought he was going to but he didn't. now we're sitting in a car with his second ex-fiancée (a garda investigating the case) who just ruined our romantic dinner

"Come on," Molly said. "Your parents used to like me."

"For the five minutes we were together in Ireland," Seamus said. "That was before you convinced me to leave the country, then left me heartbroken and alone just because I asked you to get a job."

Oof. Sorry Shay.

"That wasn't what I'd signed up for when we talked about moving to America, and you know it." Molly huffed. "It was a classic bait and switch. Plus, you know there was more to it than that."

Seamus scoffed, then turned to me.

I clicked my phone off and put it back in my clutch.

"I'm glad you did it or I wouldn't have found Shayla," Seamus said.

Molly rolled her eyes behind him, not caring to mask her disrespect. "Will you let me see the footage or not?"

"Fine," Seamus said.

I did a double-take. Had he really given in that easily? What if the footage incriminated someone in his family?

"Maybe you should ask your parents first," I said, trying not to sound guilty.

"They want to find who did this just as much as we do," Seamus said. "Even if it is a friend or family member."

I thought about my whereabouts and how they might be misconstrued on video. She'd likely notice that I wasn't with Aoife after all.

I'd have to fess up.

And then I'd probably go to jail.

20

The dress in which I'd once felt like a goddess now felt like a straitjacket.

I'd eaten too much, drank too much, and was about to be put in jail.

When we arrived at the house, Gráinne greeted us at the door with two flutes of champagne and a big smile. But her smile faltered when she saw Molly with us.

"Why is she here?" Gráinne asked, handing Seamus and me each a flute.

I resisted the urge to down mine and ask for another.

"She wants a gander at the camera footage," Seamus said. "From the night Uncle Alabaster was murdered."

"Do you know how he died?" Gráinne asked.

Molly shook her head. "The results haven't come back yet."

"But it's between the brick and the poison, right?" Seamus asked.

"It could be either of those. Or neither. We haven't yet found out." Molly crossed her arms over her chest. "Now, can we please have a look at the footage?"

This was it. I was going to jail.

Gráinne led us inside to a sitting room with a large television.

She expertly navigated to the setting for the security cameras as Donal slid onto the couch next to her.

"Usually, the man is better with these types of things," Donal said to me. "But she's the techy one in this marriage."

"I don't know why I didn't think to check the security footage. We put these things up exactly for things like this." Gráinne landed on a list of camera names. "Where should we start?"

I sipped my champagne and did my best not to cry. Maybe drinking more alcohol wasn't the best idea.

"Is there a camera in the study where Alabaster died?" Molly asked.

"Certainly not," Donal said. "That's where all the business is done."

Seamus looked at me and shook his head. Apparently, Molly didn't trust him.

"What about the hallway outside the study?" Molly asked.

Gráinne scrolled through the labeled cameras. "Here it is." She typed in the date of the party and the time the party started.

"This is the hallway leading to the study?" Molly asked, turning her head sideways to try and understand the photo.

"It's pointed at the front door," Gráinne said. "Which is just next to the door of the study."

"Right," Molly said.

We watched as people came in, were greeted by Gráinne and Donal, and then escorted into the den.

Rose walked in alone with a look of determination on her face. Gráinne gave her a big hug as they surveyed the decorations.

"Is there audio?" Molly asked.

"No," Gráinne said. "We like to have a bit of privacy in our home."

"What about the cameras outdoors? Do you keep the audio off on those as well?" Molly asked.

"No audio on those either," Gráinne said. "Would you like to keep watching this, or should we go to the outdoor ones?"

"Let's fast-forward through the introductions," Molly instructed. "We know who was at the party. We interviewed all of them."

"How did those interviews go?" I asked as Gráinne fast forwarded. "Did anyone stand out to you?"

"For now, I'm keeping my options open," Molly said. "There. Stop there."

Gráinne stopped where the hall was seemingly empty. "Did yeh see something?"

"Rewind just a bit," Molly said, scooting to the edge of the seat.

Gráinne did as she was told. The footage rewound to when Alabaster and Rose walked past the camera toward the den door.

Molly jotted a few notes in the notebook she held in front of her.

I tried to see what she'd written, but she pulled it away when she caught me looking.

"What's so important about Rose and Uncle Alabaster walking past the camera together?" Seamus asked.

"Just taking down the details," she said, glancing from him to me. She was trying to corroborate my story. And it started with me finding Alabaster and Rose in the den together. At least that part of my story checked out.

We watched as the area within the camera stayed empty until Rose went storming down the hall and out the front door.

"Was she here when you interviewed people?" I asked.

Molly didn't answer.

"Molly?" Seamus said, tension seeping through his words.

"Fine," she said. "Yes, Rose was here when we interviewed everyone. Let's move on."

Gráinne pointed the remote at the TV, but just as she was about to fast forward, Molly held up a hand.

"Hold on," Molly said as a woman walked partially into the frame.

Judging by the hand on her arm, she wasn't alone either.

"Is that Nuala?" I asked, noticing the jeweled dress.

"Yes," Gráinne said. "She's wearing that dress with all the jewels covering her private places."

"That's exactly what I was thinking," I said. "But what is she doing?"

She was flailing her arms all around. The hand previously holding onto her was now gone.

"It looks like she's arguing with someone," Seamus said. "At least that's how she used to fight with me."

"Can you rewind it a bit?" I asked Gráinne.

She did. I could feel Molly's gaze on me as I got up and walked closer to the TV. "There, can you pause it?"

The video stopped, slightly blurred.

"See that hand on her arm?" I asked. "It looks like a masculine hand."

I glanced back to see both Seamus and his father looking at their hands, probably to determine what a masculine hand looked like.

"This was right before Killian proposed," Gráinne said. "Do you think that's Killian with her?"

"Why would he propose right after they were arguing?" Molly asked.

"I don't think they were arguing," I said. "I think they were practicing."

21

"Practicing?" Molly asked, sitting up straighter and adjusting her uniform.

Seamus looked past me at the screen.

"Can you move through the footage slowly?" I asked Gráinne.

She pointed the remote at the TV. The video on the screen moved more slowly than before.

"Okay, pause," I said.

Gráinne did at the exact right moment.

"See there?" I pointed at Nuala's face. "She's smiling."

Molly tilted her head to the side. "How can you tell? All you can see is the side of her cheek."

"Come closer," I said.

Molly stood and came up next to me. "You're right, she is smiling."

"But what does that have to do with Uncle Alabaster?" Seamus asked.

"Maybe nothing," I said, trying to piece my thoughts together. "Can you keep going slowly?"

Gráinne pushed a button, and the video inched by.

We watched as Nuala's hands came to her mouth after waving her arms in the air a few more times.

I turned to Gráinne. "Are there cameras in the den?"

"Yes," she said, a smile coming over her face. She pushed a few buttons and navigated to the moment Killian had proposed to Nuala.

When she pushed play, everything came into focus. Nuala made the same motions as she had in the hallway—flailing arms, hands over mouth.

"They were practicing the proposal?" Donal asked from his position next to Gráinne.

"What does that have to do with Alabaster's death?" Molly asked.

I thought about it for a moment. "If the proposal was fake, they were likely just trying to get the ring, right?"

No one answered.

Molly looked around at Seamus and his parents. "What ring?"

"The ring that was intended for Seamus, but Killian wanted for Nuala," Gráinne finally said.

"It looks to me like Killian may not have actually wanted the ring for Nuala," I said. "If they were practicing a proposal, maybe this was just a big scheme to cash in, especially since she said the ring was hideous."

"No," Seamus said. "Killian isn't like that. He wouldn't have intentionally tried to take that ring from me. He's like me brother."

"The ring in question," Molly said, "how much is it worth exactly?"

Gráinne narrowed her eyes. "It's always about the money with you, isn't it?"

"Mam," Seamus warned.

"Don't Mam me," Gráinne said. "This girl took me baby

boy, then left him heartbroken hundreds of miles away. All because of money."

Molly sighed. "I'm simply asking because it might be a factor in the investigation. Did Alabaster give Killian the ring?"

"No. But that means nothing," Seamus said. "Killian would never hurt Uncle Alabaster."

"We can't completely rule him out," Molly said.

Seamus stood, coming eye to eye with her. "You already tried to break up me family once, and here you are doing it again."

"I'm not trying to break up your family now, and I wasn't trying to break up your family before," Molly said, not backing down in the slightest. "I'm trying to do my job. To get to the bottom of this murder. Someone killed your uncle. Someone close to your family. Close enough, they were here for your welcome home party that night."

"Fine, but it wasn't Killian," Seamus said.

I stepped between them. "That's enough. Molly, you interviewed Killian and Nuala. Did they have alibis for the time Alabaster was killed?"

Molly and Seamus didn't acknowledge me at first.

I cleared my throat.

Reluctantly, Molly took her gaze off Seamus and set it on me. "It's hard to know."

Seamus turned and walked to the other side of the room, pacing.

"Why so?" I asked.

"Everyone had alibis," she said. "But most people had one other person as their alibi. Seamus and Gráinne, you and Aoife, Killian and Nuala. That's why we need proof. Hard evidence. That's why we need to go through every bit of footage you have."

Seamus turned to pace back toward us. "Shall I put on a kettle? It sounds like it's going to be a long night."

Seamus wasn't exaggerating. We went through the rest of the front hall footage, which only showed a handful of people coming and going, usually in pairs.

The footage from the den was relatively uneventful besides when I pushed Alabaster. I hadn't realized I'd shoved him so hard. His tumble backward looked like it hurt. If only I could apologize.

Seamus squeezed my hand. "He had it coming. This is probably why he was murdered. Didn't know how to keep well enough to himself."

"You think someone murdered him because he came onto them?" Molly asked.

"It seems likely, doesn't it?" Seamus asked. "He was hitting on Rose and then Shayla and then Clara. He probably hit on everyone besides me mam."

Molly considered this for a moment.

"Did anyone else complain about Alabaster hitting on them?" I asked her. I was tired and tip-toeing around the point wasn't within my abilities anymore.

"Not directly," Molly said. "But in a case like this, it's unlikely people would offer information that would make them look suspicious."

"I did," I said. "I told you about him hitting on me."

"Did I say I suspected you?" Molly asked.

I didn't know whether she was actually trying to be nice or if she had a trick up her sleeve. "Did Clara and Rose tell you about him hitting on them?"

She didn't meet my eye. "Their stories were a bit different

than yours, but they told me about their encounters with Alabaster, yes."

"So it likely wasn't either of them." I sighed.

"Or they changed their stories after they offed him," Seamus said. "I'd bet money on it being Rose. O'course it's not Clara. She wouldn't hurt a fly."

Molly said nothing in reply.

When the silence in the room became overwhelmingly awkward, Molly finally said, "Let's see a different camera angle. Maybe the one looking the other way down the hall toward the kitchen?"

My heart leaped in my chest. If any camera caught me in the area of the study around the same time Alabaster had been killed, this was the one.

Gráinne scrolled through the different cameras before she got to the one Molly was talking about.

My pulse quickened. This camera showed everything. The door to the study, the door to the bathroom, and all the way to the kitchen. It would show me going into the bathroom, coming out, going into the study, Clara storming out, and me following after my confrontation with Alabaster.

If only I'd have gone straight after Clara, there wouldn't be any question as to whether I did it. But that bit of time it took for me to yell at Alabaster would surely make Molly think it was me.

I knotted my hands in my lap as Gráinne fast-forwarded the footage.

"Let's start there," Molly said the moment I came into view.

This was the first time I'd gone to the study—the time I'd heard Alabaster with Rose. But Molly had specifically stopped it because she'd seen me.

I thought about how long it would take for Rose to exit,

then for me to. But as the time ticked down, nothing happened.

"Fast forward a bit," Molly said.

Gráinne did.

But the screen remained unchanged. No one came or went in the hallway after my initial sighting. It was almost like the footage was frozen, except the time on the screen kept moving.

Then it hit me.

I didn't need to worry about them seeing me on the screen. Because even though they'd see me, they'd see someone else too—the killer.

My exhale came out audibly, and everyone turned to look at me.

"Is something wrong with the TV?" I asked, trying to cover my obvious sigh of relief.

"It's not the TV," Molly said, looking back at the screen. "The footage has been tampered with."

22

Gráinne stopped the footage and rewound. "That's impossible. This security system is state-of-the-art and tamper-proof."

Molly stood. "Can you please take me to your control room?"

"We don't have a control room," Gráinne said. "It's all digital."

"Who has access to the footage?" Molly asked.

"Just me, Geoffrey, and Alabaster." She glanced down at the remote in her hand. "Well, he did, anyway."

"Just the three of you?" Molly asked.

"Yes." Gráinne nodded.

"Donal?"

"Didn't want access," he said. "No need. I can't work the darn thing, anyway."

"I take it the network can be accessed with any device with internet accessibility?" Molly was thinking aloud.

"Correct." Then it was as if a lightbulb flashed on in Gráinne's head. She scrolled through the controls on the screen. "But there's a log of who was in the system. It would tell us who might have accessed the system."

Molly eased herself back onto the sofa, her gaze focused on the TV as Gráinne found the settings and the system log.

"It looks like that night both Geoffrey and Alabaster were logged in."

The code on the screen was barely recognizable. Gráinne's ability to decipher it so quickly was impressive.

"And either of them could have tampered with the camera?" Molly asked.

Gráinne thought this through for a moment. "I suppose they could have, but to be honest with you, they're both a bit dim with this stuff. They had access and logged in to spy on the staff when they suspected them of stealing or to check who was in the driveway before they answered the door. I don't think they could dupe the cameras."

"With all due respect, could you dupe the cameras?" Molly asked.

Gráinne didn't seem to take offense to this question. "I suppose if I wanted to, I could figure something out. But I wasn't logged in. And, you can ask everyone, I was busy all night with my hostess duties."

"What about since then?" Molly asked.

"As you can see, this is the first time I've logged in for more than a week," Gráinne said, though I certainly wouldn't have been able to figure that out from the screen in front of us.

Molly thought for a minute. "Did any of you share your passwords?"

"No," Gráinne said. "The man who set it up was particular about that. We were to share our information with no one. Basically, for times like these. Not that we thought something like this could have happened when we got the cameras installed."

"Do you think Uncle Alabaster did it?" Seamus whispered.

"Why would he want to alter the footage?" Gráinne asked.

"If he was taking women into his study to take advantage of them, he probably wouldn't have wanted video proof," Seamus said.

It was a solid idea.

"In your logs, does it tell what sort of device they used to access their accounts?" Molly asked.

Gráinne looked back at the screen. "Alabaster was on his cell phone, and Geoffrey was on his tablet."

"Right," Molly said. "Is there any way you might know the code to Alabaster's cell phone? We have it, but we haven't been able to get into it."

"One, Two, Three, Four," Gráinne said. "We told him it needed to be more secure, but I suppose it's rather secure in its simplicity."

Molly wrote the code down. I almost laughed. How could she forget it?

I chided myself. Who was I to question another officer of the law? If that was her way of doing things, then so be it. She'd been a Garda far longer than I'd been a police officer.

"Do you want to see any other bits of footage?" Gráinne asked.

"Will any of this footage be deleted?" Molly asked.

"Not unless I delete it," Gráinne said.

Molly stood. "Do you have any intention of deleting it?"

Gráinne thought about this for a moment, then said, "No."

"Does Geoffrey have access to delete the footage?" Molly asked.

Gráinne shook her head. "Only I do."

"Thank you for allowing me to view this." Molly took a

business card from her pocket. "If you go through any more footage and find suspicious activity, will you please call me?"

Gráinne took the card but neither agreed nor disagreed to Molly's request.

"I'll see my way out." Molly turned and left without so much as another word.

When the door clicked in place, it was as if the room exhaled.

"That was quite the spectacle," Gráinne said. "All for nothing too."

"I think we'll head to bed," Seamus said, grabbing my hand. "I'd like to take Shayla riding tomorrow if that's all right with you?"

His mother winked. "Of course it is. Poppy will be so excited to see you again."

I turned to Seamus. "Poppy?"

"My horse," Seamus said with a huge grin on his face. "I can't believe she's not gone off to see the big man in the sky by now."

"Yeh probably won't want to take her riding—take her babies—but make sure you give her some love." Gráinne had a glow when she spoke about the horses. The same glow that was currently on Seamus' face.

"We'll do that," Seamus said.

He practically skipped up the stairs like an excited little boy. "I can't believe Poppy's still alive. She was my best mate before I left. I practically raised her after her mother died giving birth. I missed all sorts of school. But in our family, horses take priority. The only thing above horses is, well, family."

I loved seeing him so passionate about something. "You really love the horses, don't you?"

He opened the door to our room. "How could you tell?"

"You light up when you talk about them. Same as your mom."

"Runs in me blood," Seamus said.

"Then why did you leave?" I asked. The question I wanted to ask got caught in my throat.

"Molly, mostly," he said, a shadow passing over his face. "But there were other factors too."

"If you don't want to tell me, you don't have to," I said. "I've just never seen this side of you before."

He ran a hand through his hair. "Let's talk more about it tomorrow."

Seamus and I had been together long enough for me to know that when he wanted to put off talking about something, we likely wouldn't end up revisiting the subject.

It also meant this subject was more delicate than I thought.

23

After a hearty breakfast, Seamus and I were on our way to the stables.

"It almost feels like we're back in the States, right?" Seamus asked as we headed down a paved path in the fanciest golf cart I'd ever seen.

"How so?" I asked. Though Colorado had lots of trees, it was nowhere near as green as Ireland. Everywhere I looked, there was green. The grass. The hills. The trees. Even in the winter, it was green.

"Being on the right side of the cart," Seamus said with a laugh.

I smiled. I was on the right, and he was driving from the left. "Was it hard to learn to drive in the States?"

"Not so much," he said. "Took some getting used to driving at all, to be honest. Growing up, we always had a driver."

I didn't know whether to laugh or be jealous. Neither seemed appropriate. "Is this all your family's property?"

"Tis," he said. "Me mam and da's. They bought out the land from Uncle Alabaster and Uncle Geoffrey before I was born."

"So your uncles only own their houses?"

"For now," he said. "Don't know what'll come of Uncle Alabaster's place now. And the castle's been sold."

"It has?" I asked. "Does Aoife know?"

He shrugged. "I'm sure her parents have told her."

I felt terrible for her. My mom still lived in the house where I grew up. It was small, but if she wanted to sell it, it would be like selling my childhood.

And this was their family castle.

A freaking castle.

"I'm surprised your family let the castle go," I said.

"Castles are a dime a dozen here," he said. "Plus, they're damp and dark, and I don't know what Aoife was thinking with those plans of hers."

Her plans had sounded pretty cool to me, but I'd never actually seen the castle. Maybe Seamus was right.

I didn't have time to push harder with my questions because rising over the hill ahead was a massive complex.

"Those're the stables," Seamus said with a proud smile.

It was so spectacular, it almost brought tears to my eyes. Four barns created a square with what looked like a courtyard in the center. "What are the buildings over there?"

"Those are the staff housing," Seamus said. "We have to have people close in case of emergencies."

It sounded like a dream job.

"I'll take you through the breeding stables to see the babies first," he said.

"Baby horses?" I hadn't considered they'd have babies. But if they bred horses, of course, they would.

"Foals," Seamus said. "You're gonna love them."

He parked the golf cart next to a couple of others that looked identical and helped me out of my seat.

I could hardly stifle my squeals as we walked into the first barn. Though, barn might have been too general a term. This was no barn. It was a spotless, concrete-floored, dark wood and black metal masterpiece.

Each of the stables had a custom, laser engraved nameplate with the mother and the baby's names and their lineage. There was no horse tack strewn about. No extra hay. Nothing.

"Hey, Seamus," a deep Irish voice greeted us from behind. "Yer mam said yeh might be coming out today."

We turned to face a giant of a man wearing a dark blue button-down shirt with the stable's logo and jeans that looked like they'd been professionally pressed and starched.

"What's the craic, Wes?" Seamus shook Wes' bear paw-sized hand.

"Divil a bit," Wes said. "And this is your lady?"

"Shayla," I said with a smile. "It's nice to meet you."

He shook my hand gently. "The pleasure is all mine."

"I'm sorry to hear about your uncle," Wes said, turning his attention back to Seamus. "He was a good man."

"No, he wasn't," Seamus said with a laugh.

"You're right. He wasn't," Wes said. "But I'm sorry, anyway. I'm sure this is giving your family quite the headache."

"Tis," Seamus said. "Murder investigation and all."

"And the will?" Wes said.

"Nothing stays secret around here, does it?" Seamus didn't seem angry that the family's personal business had been made public.

"Not unless you kill someone," Wes said.

"We'll find who did it," Seamus said. "It'll just take time."

"You'll find who did it?" Wes lifted an eyebrow and glanced at me.

I shrugged. "Molly asked for our help."

"Molly," Wes said her name as if he had bitten into something bitter. "Too bad she couldn't have moved somewhere else."

"It's no bother," Seamus said. "Can we see the foals?"

Wes's face widened into a smile. "O'course yeh can. You're the boss."

"Me mam's the boss," Seamus corrected.

Wes shrugged as if it was neither here nor there. "We had one born just last night." He led us to one of the first stables. The door was a dark wood on the bottom with black metal bars on top, leaving space to see inside.

A tiny brown foal was curled up at its mother's side, eyes closed, content.

"She's a beauty," Seamus said, then glanced at the plaque. "Good lineage too."

"She'll be a fast one," Wes said. "Might even win us a few titles."

Seamus smiled. "Do you have any we might be able to pet?"

"Sure, sure." Wes led us down to the far end of the barn.

Now and then, I'd peek into a stall to see a cute little foal with its mother.

"This little guy loves attention," Wes said as he opened the door.

The mother horse—a shiny black mare with a long white stripe down her nose—stood to the side as the little foal hopped around when he saw us. He looked just like her, only his white mark was in the shape of a heart on his forehead.

"We call him Cupid," Wes said. "He's a big lover."

Seamus let the mother horse smell his hand before he reached up and stroked her mane. "Come on in," he said to me.

I took a step into the stall, my brand-new boots sinking into the straw bed. Mirroring Seamus, I let the mare smell my outstretched hand. I held my breath as she took a step toward me.

Seamus put a hand on my back, urging me to hold my position.

I did.

When she ducked her head to let me wind my fingers through her mane, I exhaled with a smile.

"Looks like Whinny likes you," Wes said, stroking cupid's back. "She doesn't like many women."

"Shayla's not just any woman," Seamus said. "She's special."

24

We played with Cupid and Whinny for a few minutes before Seamus showed me around the rest of the compound. It was just as beautiful and impeccably maintained.

"I can see why the business is so successful," I said. "This place is gorgeous."

"It's always been great," Seamus said. "But me mam's done wonders to improve the status. We breed some of the fastest racehorses in Ireland."

"And some of the sweetest," I said. "Cupid and Whinny are the most adorable things on the planet."

"Just wait until you meet Poppy." Seamus opened the door of the only barn we hadn't been through.

The minute Seamus stepped into view of Poppy, she went crazy. She stomped the ground, let out loud neighs, and even reared on her back legs a couple of times.

"Slow down, old girl." Seamus laughed. "You're gonna hurt yourself."

He slid open the stall door and slipped inside, obviously unafraid of the massive horse. When he reached out a hand, it almost looked like she melted into his touch. Soon enough, he had his arms wrapped around her neck. They stayed like that long enough to make me tear up.

When he let her go, he wiped a tear from his own eye. "It's so good to see you."

She pressed her forehead to his chest while he scratched her behind the ears.

"There's someone I'd like you to meet."

Why was I more nervous about meeting his horse than I had been to meet his family?

I took a tentative step forward.

"This is Shayla—the woman I'm—uh—in love with," he said.

Poppy looked me over, unsure.

"Hi Poppy," I said, slowly raising a hand to her nose. "It's nice to meet you."

She sniffed me loudly, her breaths coming out of her large nostrils in puffs of steam.

Then, all at once, she reared back and started neighing.

I'd always loved horses, but that was from afar.

"Poppy, settle down," Seamus said, his voice calm.

I took a step back as Poppy came back to rest on all four hooves.

"Is she—did I make her upset?" I asked.

Seamus laughed. "Nah, she was just excited to meet you. Go ahead. She'll let you pet her now."

I didn't have to step toward her. She came to me and placed her forehead in the middle of my chest, letting me rub behind her ears like she had with Seamus.

Seamus let out a loud laugh. "See there? I knew the two of you would be instant friends."

I stayed with her for a long time. I wasn't about to let Seamus' beloved horse down by not petting her until she was completely exhausted of it.

"I hear you have some babies we could take on a ride," Seamus said. "Mam says you were a model mother."

Poppy lifted her head from my chest and shook it, her mane flopping back and forth.

"Not that I suspected you wouldn't be," Seamus quickly added, as if his words may have offended her. "We'll find them. But we'll stop in and say goodbye before we leave."

Poppy took a step toward the door, effectively blocking us from getting out of the stall.

"Now, Poppy, enough of these silly games," Seamus said. "You best be moving so I can take Shayla on our date."

Poppy didn't budge. She stared back at him, matching his intense glare.

I almost laughed. They had quite the connection.

He tried pushing her out of the way, but she still didn't move. Finally, he said, "Be that way. We'll take you with us. But I'm not riding you, you old hag."

She stepped out of the way and let us pass.

"She's a bit stubborn," he said, smiling at me. "But she means well."

He worked on getting two of Poppy's offspring—Bentley and Matilda—ready for us to ride. I watched as he effortlessly raised the pads and then the saddles to their backs. Slipped bits in their mouths and adjusted the reins. His apparent knowledge and ease in the stables was downright sexy.

"All right," Seamus said. "Do you need help getting up there?"

"I just put my foot in the stirrup and whip my leg around, right?" I asked. "Like on the mechanical bull?"

Seamus laughed. "Yep, pretty much."

"I think I can manage," I said. Matilda was dark brown, just like Poppy. Bentley was much larger than Matilda and was a lighter shade of brown. I slipped my boot into Matilda's stirrup and pushed up, swinging my leg over her back effortlessly.

"You made that look easy," Seamus said. "Those mechanical bulls taught you well."

I laughed. "Let's just hope she doesn't buck me off being as there're no mats on the ground to catch me."

"If she's like her mom, she'll do just about anything to keep you safe."

He swung himself up into Bentley's saddle and took Poppy's lead attached to a simple halter in his left hand.

"Matilda will likely stay next to Bentley, but if you need to change her course, remember what I taught you about the reins."

I nodded. Sure enough, Matilda walked right next to Bentley, sandwiching Seamus between Poppy and me.

Seamus was a natural on a horse. He closed his eyes as we made our way out of the stables, and the sunshine hit his face.

The sun felt rather nice. I pulled on my brand-new sunglasses. Gráinne had insisted I get two pairs—one for horseback riding and one for fancier occasions. That way I didn't worry if the ones I had on got damaged when we were riding. I smiled at the memory of our shopping spree.

As Seamus and I rode in silence, my mind drifted to the case, going over every clue.

I'd only been gone a maximum of fifteen minutes while I was looking for Clara. Who I'd never actually found. She could easily be a suspect, though Molly didn't seem to think so.

And Rose was definitely a suspect. Between what I'd overheard from the den, what Alabaster had told me, and what the women at the pub had talked about, she had motive. If she truly had wanted to be with him, and he turned her down, she might have gotten angry.

We needed to talk to her.

And Clara.

And probably Killian and Nuala, too.

Plus, how had the video been erased? Or rather, recorded over? Was Alabaster trying to hide something, or was someone else?

"Doing okay over there?" Seamus asked.

I jolted at his voice, startled from my thoughts. "Just thinking about the case."

"Today is not about the case." He smiled. "Today is about us. About this beautiful day."

He was right. I didn't need to stress about a case I wasn't even technically supposed to be helping with. And now that someone had tampered with the footage, it was unlikely they'd suspect me of doing anything. Especially if Aoife kept her side of the bargain with our alibi.

But what if Aoife—

"Shayla," Seamus said. "Stop thinking about it. It'll all be settled, eventually."

25

We rode for what felt like both an eternity and a single moment. Seamus told me all about his childhood. Racing Aoife, Killian, Clara, and Nuala through the woods on horseback, exploring all the nooks and crannies of the castle, and growing up almost as siblings. The Fab Five.

I'd always thought Seamus and I were rather alike since we were both only children. But though he may have been an only child by blood, he absolutely did not grow up alone.

"Shall we take a break and have some lunch?" Seamus asked when we emerged from the trees into a grassy clearing. For being winter, the weather was relatively warm.

While Seamus tied the horses loosely to a fencepost, I laid out the heavy blanket and food Magella had arranged for us.

"You're so beautiful," Seamus said as he poured me a glass of wine. The glasses were shatterproof, according to Magella. She had been very eager to tell me all about them.

"Thank you," I said, accepting his compliment. "It helps that I've practically had a makeover since coming here."

"Nah. You're just as beautiful as the day I met you."

I smiled and sipped my wine. It was tart and sweet at the same time. "This has been a wonderful day."

"The day's not over yet." He reached into his pocket, fumbling to find something.

I sucked in a breath. Was he looking for a ring?

This was the perfect place to propose.

When his hand emerged holding his cell phone, I did my best not to show my disappointment.

He turned on a song and stood. "Would you dance with me?"

I took his outstretched hand and rose to my feet. "It would be my pleasure."

The song was an old one. Something Seamus would have listened to in high school while I was barely in elementary school.

Sometimes when I thought about our age gap, it freaked me out. Every time I brought it up, Rylie would tell me it didn't matter. I'd never really talked to Seamus about it, but he didn't seem to mind.

We danced until the song was finished.

Seamus kissed me slowly and passionately. I rose on my tiptoes, wrapping my arms more tightly around his neck.

Then he slipped out of my grasp. When I looked down, he was kneeling, trying to get something out of his jacket pocket.

But before he could, the horses started freaking out.

Poppy reared up on her back legs, letting out a loud neigh.

Seamus was back to a stand within milliseconds. Before I could ask what was wrong, he darted toward her. "Poppy, what is it?"

He didn't make it in time.

Poppy's lead came loose from the fence, and she galloped off into the trees.

I chased Seamus as he charged after her.

The other two horses stomped their feet and neighed angrily.

Instead of going after Seamus, I stopped to calm them.

Then I heard a scream.

"Seamus?" I called out. "Are you okay?"

Another scream.

The horses started pulling against their ties. I didn't want them to hurt themselves, but Seamus was out there and could need help at this very moment.

"Shhhh," I said. "It's okay. It's okay."

They stopped tugging.

I contemplated whether to untie them or leave them there.

Just as I was about to untie them and lead them into the woods with me, Seamus came walking back out with Poppy on his heels.

"What happened?"

Seamus had a big grin on his face. "Good ol Poppy." He reached back to pat her on the nose. "She never did like paparazzi."

"Paparazzi? Out here?" I looked more closely at the trees but didn't see anything.

"They're everywhere," he said. "I should have known they'd follow us. But Poppy chased them off, didn't you, girl?"

I laughed. "She really is something."

"I'm impressed you got these two to settle down after all the ruckus she caused."

"They're good kids," I said. "Just like their mama."

Matilda neighed happily and nuzzled into my side.

"I suppose we should head back anyway," Seamus said, his cheerful voice replaced with disappointment. "It looks like the snow is coming in."

I glanced up at the sky to see gray clouds in the distance.

The ride back was far too short. I could have stayed in the saddle all day. Though the minute I stepped back onto solid ground, an ache traveled up the insides of my legs. With every step I took, I felt like I was walking bow-legged.

One of the staff said she'd take care of getting the horses cleaned up and put back in their stables for the night.

We each gave all three horses an abundance of love and a couple of apples before walking hand-in-hand back to the golf cart.

Just as we were pulling onto the path, the snow started to fall.

"It's so beautiful here," I said. "The green mixed with the snow. It's like a fairytale."

"We don't get much snow down here," Seamus said. "This might be the first white Christmas I've had since me childhood."

"Do you ever think about moving back?" I asked, the words tumbling from my mouth before I could stop them.

Why had I asked that?

What if he did want to come back?

Did I want to live in Ireland?

Would he want me to come with him?

It had looked like he was going to propose, but maybe I was mistaking the situation.

"When I'm here, I do," he said. "That's probably why I don't visit much."

I nodded and waited for him to continue.

"I miss me parents. And Killian. Aoife and Clara too, but not as much. And the horses. I miss the horses."

"But you don't want to take over the family business?" So much for me staying quiet.

"I never told anyone I didn't want to. They assumed when I left that was the case."

"So you do want to?"

Seamus reached over and squeezed my hand. "What if I did? What would become of us?"

I gulped, trying to keep my nerves calm. "I suppose that would be up to you."

He stopped the golf cart in front of his parents' house and turned to face me. "I could never make such a decision for you. Someone once made that decision for me, and though it turned out better than I could have ever imagined, I would never do the same for someone else. No matter how much I loved them and wanted them to be with me."

"Are you saying you'd want me to come with you if you did decide to move back?"

He looked at me as if I'd spoken gibberish. "Well, o'course I would. Are yeh crazy?"

I laughed, giddiness rising inside me. "Then I'd come."

"Just like that?" He searched me for a sign of deception. "You'd leave the police force? Your mam? Rylie? You'd give it all up to live here with me?"

"I mean, yeah," I said, shocked that I'd practically just agreed to move to another country without so much as a thought. "I love you. I'd want to be with you if you wanted to be with me."

"Oh, I want to be with you," he said. "Every day for the rest of my—"

"How many times do I have to tell yeh to get a room?" Killian laughed. He and Nuala had somehow snuck up behind us.

"We'll finish this discussion later," Seamus said, kissing me quickly on the cheek. "Right now, we need to have a word with the two of you."

Seamus hopped out of the golf cart and wrapped an arm around Killian's shoulders. "Did yeh off Uncle Alabaster?"

26

"**S**orry?" Killian gaped at Seamus. "You think I killed our uncle?"

Seamus dropped his arm from Killian's shoulder. "Why not? You were right mad he didn't give you that ring."

"Can we talk about this inside?" Nuala asked, her teeth chattering. Snow was gathering in her hair. She wore all white, the pants tight against her thin legs, and the top sheer enough she could probably feel the snowflakes soaking through.

"Did you walk over here?" I asked, glancing down at her stilettos, then at the lack of a car in the driveway.

"It's not far to the castle," Killian said, seemingly unfazed that his girlfriend was freezing her tail off.

"Let's go inside," Seamus agreed.

Once in the kitchen, Seamus made everyone tea.

Nuala and I sat at the small table in front of a roaring fireplace while Killian leaned against the breakfast bar island.

"Where were the two of you?" Nuala asked.

"We went for a ride and then a picnic," I said, not giving her too many details, being as though she was Seamus' ex.

"He introduce you to that nasty old horse of his?"

"You couldn't possibly be talking about Poppy."

"That's the one." She examined her pointed nails. "She's a right wench if you ask me."

"She liked Shayla," Seamus said as he placed two teacups in front of us.

"Of course she did," Nuala said.

Seamus and Killian sat at the table with their own teacups.

"Now, tell me, did you kill Uncle Alabaster?" Seamus asked again.

Killian took a sip of his tea, then returned the tiny porcelain cup to its saucer. "I did not. Though, I'm not sad to see him gone."

"And why is that?" Seamus asked. "His life—or death—really has no bearing over you."

"Doesn't it?" Killian asked.

Nuala snickered.

"What is it you're not telling me?" Seamus stared at Killian, ignoring Nuala.

"Uncle may have had the intention of changing his will, but he never got around to signing it," Killian said.

"And how would you know that?" Seamus took a sip of his tea.

"I have my ways," he said. "But you can't tell anyone I told you. I only just found out yesterday. If the police know I know, they'll think I killed him because of his will."

"And what exactly does the will state?" Seamus asked.

I sipped my tea, trying to keep my hands steady.

"It splits the money equally between you, me, and Aoife, just as he always promised."

"What about your parents?" I blurted out.

"What about them?" Killian narrowed his eyes. "They got

themselves into the mess they're in. They should have to get themselves out."

"You think Uncle Alabaster left all of his money to the three of us? After all the problems he's had with us these past few years?" Seamus shook his head. "I think you're sorely mistaken."

Killian shrugged. "We'll know soon enough."

"Is the solicitor coming?" Seamus asked.

"After the holiday for sure, though, we've put in a request for him to come sooner."

Seamus didn't look happy about this information. Not in the least.

"Where were the two of you when Uncle Alabaster was killed?" Seamus asked.

"We were cooling off after the humiliation of the proposal," Nuala said.

"Killian ran off after Uncle Alabaster," Seamus said. "And you disappeared into the crowd."

"Uncle Alabaster shut the door in my face when I tried to talk to him," Killian said.

"I tried to talk to him too," Nuala said. "Just like I told Shayla. But he was in his office making out with some bimbo."

I really wanted to break the news to her that the bimbo Alabaster was making out with was likely her own mother. But that didn't seem necessary at the moment.

"I suppose congratulations on your engagement are in order," I said. "I didn't have a chance to say it before."

I could see Seamus turn to me from the corner of my eye, but I didn't meet his gaze.

"Does it look like there's a ring on my finger?" Nuala asked, holding up her left hand. "There's nothing to congratulate."

"But does one really need a ring to propose?" I asked.

"Isn't it simply a formality on top of the love two people share?"

Nuala laughed. "You can tell yourself whatever helps you sleep at night."

"But the two of you are happy and in love, right?" I asked.

Seamus smiled. He was catching on.

"I don't know," Nuala said. "Are we?" Her question was directed at Killian.

"Of course we are," Killian said. "Why else would I propose?"

"So you did propose? For real?" Nuala asked, her eyes widening.

"Yeah, Killian, did yeh? For real?" Seamus asked, his voice on the verge of teasing.

"Why're yeh asking me such stupid questions," Killian said.

"Maybe because we saw the camera footage of Nuala practicing her reaction to your proposal," Seamus said.

Nuala's eyes widened. "I didn't—why would you think—"

"You don't need to lie to us," I said. "We saw it on the recording."

Nuala looked at Killian to save her.

He sighed. "Fine, it doesn't matter anyway now that the truth about the will has come out. Nuala and I are dating. But only casually. When I found out Uncle Alabaster changed his will, I knew the only way to get a piece of my rightful inheritance was by going for the ring. I'm surprised you didn't try it since the two of you seem so . . . close."

Seamus didn't reply.

"I promised her a cut of the money we'd make from the ring if she'd go along with the proposal," Killian said.

Seamus looked like someone had slapped him across the face.

"So now what?" I asked. "Are you going to get a cut of his inheritance?"

Nuala crossed her arms over her chest. "I don't know." She looked at Killian. "Am I?"

Killian shrugged.

Nuala stood. "This is such a waste of my time."

Killian didn't even try to stop her as she stormed out of the room, the front door slamming shut behind her.

"That was harsh," Seamus said.

Killian looked directly at me when he said, "It's what she gets for being a gold digger."

I was about to defend myself when Donal burst into the kitchen. "Come quick. It's your mother."

27

Gráinne was sitting in front of the TV in the exact position and clothes she had been in the night before.

"Has she moved at all?" Seamus asked.

"Not all night," Donal said. "She keeps going through the footage, trying to find something."

"Mam?" Seamus asked, approaching her as if she was a mama moose with a baby nearby.

"I'm fine," Gráinne said, her voice gravelly. "I'm almost through it. There has to be something here."

Seamus looked from his mother to his father and then to me.

"Hey," I said. "Why don't we finish going through everything after a nap and some food? You'll have fresh eyes and—"

"There," she said as if she hadn't heard me speaking. "It's right there. Who is that?"

She pointed at the screen, and we all turned.

It was an outdoor shot of the steps leading up to the front door. A person lurked in the bushes on the far side of the drive.

"Whoever it is probably threw the brick," Gráinne said, pushing play.

The sound of wind blared through the sound system around the room.

Seamus, Killian, Donal, and I covered our ears while Gráinne just sat and watched, unfazed by the noise.

Donal grabbed a different remote from the stand and turned the volume down.

Still, Gráinne did nothing but watch unblinkingly at the footage. "Where did he go?"

The figure was no longer in the bushes.

"Maybe it was a photographer trying to get a shot," Seamus said. "They've been out in force lately."

"It wasn't a photographer," Gráinne said. "There he is again."

The person's head popped up from behind the bushes. He moved up the driveway toward the front of the house.

"He has a brick in his hand," Gráinne said.

"And a limp," I said. The limp looked familiar. Had I noticed it at the party?

The person wore all black, including a mask over their face. "It could be a woman."

"Do you think it is?" Gráinne asked.

"We just don't want to rule anything out."

Seamus smiled at me. Killian rolled his eyes.

The person raised the brick as if to throw it, then stopped and practically dove into the bushes. Had someone seen them through the office window? I glanced at the time stamp on the recording.

Alabaster would die within a matter of minutes.

The person stood again, took a second to look in the window, then threw the brick. The minute glass shattered, the person ran away, the limp more pronounced with every step.

"Do you recognize that limp?" I asked.

"Do you know how many people in town have a limp?" Killian asked. "It would be like asking if we recognized someone because they were six feet tall. Plus, people don't like it when others gawk at their limps."

"Six feet tall is pretty tall, though," Donal said. "Probably more likely to identify someone by their height than by their limp."

I considered this. Maybe for someone who lived there and saw people limping all the time. But this one had a very distinctive pattern. It was a half step left, then a drag right, half step left, drag right.

"I think it's Harry," I said. "He was limping like that the other day when we were at his pub."

Gráinne and the others stared as the man limped down the drive and out of view.

"She's right, yeh know. Harry has a gammy leg," Seamus said. "Maybe it's because we've not been here to observe all the limps, but that right there's Harry's limp if I ever did see it."

"Did you invite him to the party?" Donal asked.

Gráinne shook her head. "Didn't think he'd come. He's always so busy with the pub. Plus, you know he's been having problems with me brother."

"Alabaster?" I asked.

She shook her head. "No, no. Geoffrey."

"Did I hear me name?" Geoffrey walked into the room dressed as if he was going to a fancy dinner party.

Killian groaned at the sight of his father.

"It's a pleasure to see you again, Shayla." Geoffrey held out a hand to take mine, then raised it to his lips and kissed the back gently.

"Come off it, da," Killian said. "Laying the charm on a little thick, aren't ya?"

"Just because you don't like the girl doesn't mean I can't," Geoffrey snapped, then returned his gaze to me and smiled. "Did you have a nice time riding today?"

"I did," I said. He may have been similar to a smarmy car salesman, but there was something about him that was magnetic.

"Grand, that's grand," Geoffrey said. "Why are yeh watching security footage of Harry traipsing around in the bushes?"

Geoffrey had to have been watching from the doorway because, by the time he'd come in, Harry had gone off the screen.

"Yeh think that's who it is?" Gráinne said.

"No question in me mind," Geoffrey said. "Suppose the brick's what killed Alabaster?"

"If so," Seamus said, "Harry would be our killer."

Except for the sprig of mistletoe across his lips. It had to have been placed there after he'd fallen—after he was dead.

And if Harry ran—or rather, limped—away, there was no way he would have had time to sneak back in to do that before I went into the office. But only the Gardaí and I knew about the mistletoe.

"Can you keep the footage playing a bit?" I asked.

Gráinne pushed play, and we watched as basically nothing happened. A muffled ruckus came from inside the house, presumably because Alabaster had just been found dead.

"Can you rewind it to before he threw the brick?" I asked.

Gráinne did.

He snuck up the driveway again. Half step, drag, half step, drag. He looked around, ready to throw the brick but then dove into the bushes.

"Sorry," I said. "Can you rewind it for me again and play it back more slowly?"

We watched as he raised his hand in slow motion, holding the brick high. "There. Did you see that?" I pointed at the screen.

Everyone looked at me with confused stares.

"He glances over his shoulder," I said. "Something spooked him from around the side of the house."

Gráinne replayed the video and, this time, they saw it.

"You're right," Seamus said. "Someone was over there."

"Is there a door that leads that way from the house?" I asked.

"Someone could have gone out the back, through the kitchen and around," Geoffrey said.

But the looks on Killian and Seamus' faces told me there was more to the story.

"What aren't you saying?" I asked.

"There's a secret passageway," Seamus said.

"Yeh wanker, you're not supposed to tell anyone," Killian objected.

"We made that pact when we were ten," Seamus said. "This is a matter of murder."

"Please tell me it doesn't lead out of the office," I said.

"Not the office," Seamus said. "The bookcase on the other side of the bathroom door."

Killian groaned.

"How many people know it's there?" I asked.

Seamus shrugged. "No idea? When we were kids, we thought only the five of us knew."

"The Fab Five?"

"Right," he said. "But surely our parents and the staff and the builders and probably a handful of other people knew too."

Gráinne, Donal, and Geoffrey nodded.

"Maybe we should go check it out," I said. "See if someone might have accessed it that night and left behind a clue."

"Before we do that," Gráinne stood and looked at her brother. "I need to know why you were tampering with the video footage."

28

Geoffrey took a step back, nearly knocking over a tall decorative vase. He quickly steadied it before looking back at Gráinne. "I didn't alter any of the footage."

"You and Alabaster were the only two signed in to the system that evening. Alabaster was here all night. That leaves you." Gráinne, though much smaller and younger than Geoffrey, made him practically cower at her voice.

"It wasn't me," Geoffrey said. "I lost the tablet I use months ago. It has me login information stored in it. I wouldn't even know how to access the files without my tablet."

"Why didn't you tell someone you lost your tablet?" Gráinne said.

"I told Shannon," Geoffrey mumbled. "She said it would turn up. It's so small, though, it could easily be stuck between a cushion in the sofa."

"Do you think she has it?" Gráinne asked.

He shook his head. "She wouldn't know what to do with it if she did. She's as bad with electronics as Donal."

"So we have a missing tablet with access to the video footage, a secret passageway the killer may have escaped through, and a whole handful of guests who loathed Uncle Alabaster," Killian said. "Sounds like we're making serious progress on this case."

His sarcasm lit a fire under me. "We're uncovering facts. Eventually, the pieces will fit together."

Killian shrugged. "Fit them together then. In the meantime, I'm going home. I need to change the locks before Nuala cleans me out."

He walked out of the room.

"Shall we go look at this secret passage?" I asked.

I didn't want to lose steam at this point.

"Secret passage?" A woman's voice came from the doorway. "Killian let me in on his way out." Molly studied the television. "Who is that?"

"Harry from the pub," Geoffrey said. "He's your killer."

"Is that right?" Molly looked at me for confirmation.

Validation flowed through me. She seemed to be asking my professional opinion. "I'm not so sure."

Seamus frowned at me. "You're not?"

"How about you show Molly and me that secret passageway?" I said, grabbing his hand and leading him to the doorway where Molly stood.

"Mam," Seamus said, turning back to her, "you should get some rest now. We have this handled, okay?"

She slumped back in the chair as if she just realized she'd been awake over twenty-four hours.

"I'll get her to bed," Donal said.

Geoffrey followed us out of the room and then let himself out the front door. "I need to catch up with Killian. I'll talk with you again soon."

We walked down the hall to the bookcase set into the wall right next to the bathroom door. Directly on the other side of the bathroom was the study, meaning if someone killed Alabaster, they could have gone through the study door leading to the bathroom, then snuck out and through the passageway after I went into the study.

Even if people had seen someone come out of the bathroom, they likely wouldn't have thought anything of it. Not at the time, anyway.

"It's the elephant," Seamus said, showing Molly and me. "You pull its trunk down, and the bookcase swings into the wall."

Molly took a flashlight from her belt and shone it into the dark space. "Before I go in, what was all that back there? Why don't you think Harry was the one who did this? If it's apparent he threw the brick—the brick that could have killed Alabaster?"

"He may have thrown the brick. And, though I doubt it, it could have killed him. But someone else had to be in the office," I said. "The mistletoe couldn't have been on his mouth when he got hit in the head with the brick."

"Wait," Seamus said. "He had mistletoe in his mouth?"

"On his mouth," I said. "It was in perfect shape, laid across his lips. Almost like—"

"A warning," Seamus said.

"Or a signature," Molly said. "That does complicate things. Between you and me, and this can't go anywhere, the drink on Alabaster's desk was poisoned. The lab is still running the report, and the autopsy will take a while longer, but I'd bet he died by poisoning before I'd bet he died by that brick."

She stepped into the dark hole, and Seamus and I followed.

I had always wanted a secret passageway in my house growing up. Seamus was so lucky to have called this his home.

My heart rate quickened. This could eventually be my kids' grandparents' home. My kids—our kids—could have secret passageways to wander through.

Then a pang tugged at me. I'd be leaving Rylie. And my mom.

Not that I had the best relationship with my mother, but she was still the only family I had.

And leaving the police department—a job I'd worked so hard to get—would be tough, too. Though I wouldn't miss the comparisons and the coffee-getting.

"Hold up," Molly said. "Look right here."

She shone her flashlight at what looked like a clump of blonde hair. Long blonde hair.

Both Seamus and Molly turned to look at me, then at my hair.

I held my hands up. "I've never been in here before. I swear."

Molly photographed the hair and then collected it in an evidence bag. "If we can trace the DNA, we might be able to decipher who did this."

"That's assuming whoever did this came through this passageway," I said.

"Of course," Molly agreed.

"Do you smell that?" I asked.

"Damp dirt?" Seamus said.

"I think it's cigarette smoke." I sniffed. "It's faint, but it's there."

"I smell it too," Molly said. "Who smokes?"

"Nuala," I said. "I saw her smoking in the garden earlier that night."

"Nuala doesn't have long blonde hair, though," Seamus said. "Not that I'm defending her," he added quickly when the two of us turned to look at him at the same time.

"Anyone else smoke?" Molly asked.

Seamus shook his head. "No one I know."

Molly started back down the tunnel and, within a few steps, reached a dead end.

Seamus walked in front of us. "To get out, you just turn the handle and push the door open."

The door opened out to the side of the house and was hidden behind a massive shrub. The door was also the same color and texture as the house from the outside, so it blended perfectly when closed.

"How do you get back in?" I asked.

"There's a rock." He kicked it with his shoe. "If you push it over, the door unlatches, and you just have to pull right here." He pointed to a small handle camouflaged in the door's texture.

Molly looked around before we fully walked outside.

Just as we were coming to the end of the hedge, she stopped us and put a finger to her lips.

I peeked around her to see Killian and Geoffrey in what looked to be a heated argument.

"You lost your tablet, da?" Killian shouted. "Lying to the police on top of everything else won't help your case, you know?"

"I did lose it," Geoffrey said.

"Right," Killian said. "You and I both know who has it. And if you don't tell the police soon, I will."

"Fine, I'll tell them," Geoffrey said. "But what about the money, son? Are you going to help your dear old mam and da out?"

Killian looked like he might spit in his father's face. "I will never give you money again as long as I live." Killian slipped into his driver's seat and slammed the car door in Geoffrey's face.

Killian sped off down the driveway as Geoffrey stood watching.

"Can you tell us a bit about that conversation?" Molly asked as she walked up behind Geoffrey.

"My son despises me." Geoffrey looked genuinely hurt by his son's words. "It's not something I'm proud of."

"Why does he despise you?" Molly asked.

"You're that girl who convinced Seamus to run away to America," Geoffrey said.

Molly didn't act taken aback in the slightest. "Not one of my finer moments."

"And this is not one of mine," Geoffrey said. "Now, if you'll excuse me?"

"One more question," Molly said. "Who really has the tablet?"

29

Geoffrey stood staring at Molly long enough to make it awkward.

"Just answer her question," Seamus said. "The sooner we find out, the sooner we can figure out who killed Uncle Alabaster."

"You think whoever has my tablet killed Alabaster?" Geoffrey laughed as if this was an impossibility.

"You don't?" I asked.

"I don't know what Killian was going on about," Geoffrey said. "I lost my tablet ages ago. When it happened, I honestly didn't think about the surveillance access. I highly doubt wherever that tablet is, anyone accessed the surveillance footage."

"The log says you were in the system the night of the murder," Molly said.

"I never log out of the system on the tablet," Geoffrey said. "Trust me, if I ever find it, the first thing I'll do is log out so I don't end up getting hassled by the guards again."

"My intention is not to hassle you," Molly said in a

completely professional tone. "My intention is to find out who killed your brother."

"That's the question of the hour, isn't it?" Geoffrey stared down the empty driveway. "Whoever did it wasn't doing anyone any favors. No matter how much they might have thought they were."

I looked at Seamus, who shrugged.

"If you were leading this investigation," I said, "who would you question first?"

Geoffrey didn't take his gaze off the horizon when he said, "Probably the person who has the most to gain from his death."

"And that would be?" I asked gently.

"Me," he said, his voice barely above a whisper. "At least that's what you'd think as an outsider. You'd think Alabaster would leave his wealth to his more immediate family—his sister and brother—rather than his niece and nephews. Though I suppose if someone knew about him passing me up, they might think I killed him out of anger. So, again, it would be me."

"Did you kill your brother?" I whispered.

He dropped his head. "I wasn't even at the party."

That wasn't an answer. "If someone gave you that answer when you were investigating, what would you think?"

"That they weren't answering my question," Geoffrey said, turning his gaze toward me and flashing me a smile. "You're one smart cookie."

His charm wouldn't work on me. He was hiding something. "Did you kill him?"

"No," he said, not flinching, not taking his piercing gaze from mine, not giving any indication of lying. "I didn't kill Alabaster."

"If you didn't, who did?" I asked.

He turned his gaze back to the horizon. "I'm not sure."

Molly, Seamus, and I went back inside when Geoffrey left in his fancy sports car.

"Are there any other secret passages in the house you'd like to tell me about?" Molly asked Seamus.

He shook his head. "No."

I didn't know whether he was saying no because there were none or because he didn't want to tell her about them.

"Have you come across anything else?" she asked.

"Were we supposed to?" I asked. "I thought you didn't want us helping unless given express permission."

She sighed. "I'm sure that hasn't stopped you. I know all about your friend, Rylie, and her antics in the States. I've seen the YouTube videos."

"I can assure you, I am not Rylie," I said. "However, the difference between Rylie and me is that I am an actual police officer. Rylie is not. But she is respected by many in my department. She's solved more crimes—in an unorthodox fashion, sure—than several of our detectives."

"Shayla likes to do things by the book," Seamus said.

Molly's phone chimed from her pocket. She pulled it out and frowned at whatever message was on the screen. "I have to go." She stood. "If you come across anything, let me know."

"Are you giving us permiss—"

She cut me off. "If you come across anything, let me know."

When she was gone, I looked at Seamus.

"That's about as close to permission as we're gonna get," Seamus said. "Where do we start?"

"You start by telling me about the other hidden passage-ways in your house," I said. "It must have been so much fun growing up here."

Seamus laughed. "I'm happy to show you every secret about this house, just as soon as we get a proper meal in me stomach."

"Magella had to leave early," Donal said, coming into the kitchen. "Why don't the two of you go into town? Your mother showed her the swanky side. Why don't you show her the other side?"

Seamus' face lit up. "That's a grand idea. What do you say?"

"I'd like to change out of my riding gear first," I said. "But then, absolutely. I'd love to see the other side."

30

This was definitely another side of Ballywick. Where Gráinne had shown me the cute little row of boutiques right in the center of town, Seamus took me off the beaten path.

He had driven us himself, which had been hilarious as he tried to remember to stay on the left side of the road. At least, it had been hilarious until we almost hit another car head-on.

It was strange holding his hand from the left side of the vehicle. As we drove through what I figured were more of the outskirts of the town, I saw children playing in their yards, sheep behind rock walls, each of them with a painted marker on their backs, and a school with a sign that said: Closed for the Holiday.

"That's where I went to school as a wee lad," Seamus said. "Rode the bus every day with Killian, Aoife, Clara, and Nuala until Clara was old enough to drive herself. That's around the time the Fab Five broke up. Being a seventeen-year-old girl, I can imagine why she didn't want to hang out with a bunch of kids."

"How much older is she?" I asked.

"When she was seventeen, Killian, Nuala, and I were twelve. Aoife was ten."

That was quite the gap at those ages.

"She was such a mother hen, Clara was," Seamus said with a smile. "Just like her own mother."

"Where is her father?" I asked.

"He died before she was born," Seamus said.

"That's too bad." I'd never met my father either. Though he wasn't dead. At least, I didn't think he was. From the stories Mother told, I was better off without him.

Seamus squeezed my hand. "This is the place." He pulled the car into a parking spot in front of a thatched cottage in a row of several. This one had a sign out front that said: Ballywick Café.

He got out and rushed to my side of the car to open the door for me. I'd put on a pair of my new blue jeans and a blue cashmere sweater Gráinne had insisted made my eyes pop.

"Aren't cafés usually mostly breakfast?" I asked. We were solidly into dinner time and closely bordering on pub time.

"We're not going to the café," he said with a mischievous grin on his face. "Come on."

I took his hand, and we walked through a narrow passage between the café and what looked like a flower shop.

When we almost reached the alleyway behind the two, Seamus knocked on a side door leading into the same building the café was in.

There was no sign—no indication—this was anything other than a side door leading to the café.

When the door swung open, the man simply let us inside. No fumbling over his words when he saw Seamus, no trying to impress. It was a breath of fresh air after all the coddling people had done in his and Gráinne's presences while in town.

The inside was dark and moody, somewhat like the pub, but with dim twinkle lights. Whether they were supposed to be dim or they'd almost run their course, I didn't know, but either way, it made the atmosphere homey and edgy.

A small stage sat on the wall that neighbored the café, and an Irish band played a slow, melancholy song.

"What'll yeh be havin'?" the man who let us in asked in a gruff voice.

"A draft for me," Seamus said. "And a burger."

I glanced over at the small bar where the only thing on tap was Guinness. "I'll have the same, please."

He didn't reply, just shrugged and walked away.

"This place is amazing," I said. "How did you find it?"

"It's one of many holes in the wall. Livin' here yeh find 'em pretty easily. Some come and go, but this one's been here since I can remember."

"I think it's the first time we've been anywhere in Ireland where people aren't staring at us," I said.

"Everyone keeps to themselves in places like these." Seamus reached across the table and took my hand. "I'm so glad you came here with me."

"Well, I was hungry, so . . ."

"Not here, here," he said with a chuckle. "Here as in Ireland. Ballywick."

I laughed. "I know. I'm just codding ya."

His eyes widened. "Good one! Yer gettin' the lingo down already."

He rubbed a thumb over the top of my hand. "When we were talking before, about moving here. Were yeh serious?"

"I was," I said. "I am. It'll be a change. I'll miss Rylie and my mom, but I want to be where you are. And I've never seen you as happy as you are here. I can tell you love your family and miss them tremendously."

"That I do."

"Why did you really leave? What factors were there other than Molly?"

His face dropped. "I suppose I should tell ya. It's not that I've been hiding it, exactly. It's just hard to talk about. And no one else knows. No one but Molly and me."

I wasn't sure where this was going. Had they committed some sort of crime and had to flee?

I laughed internally at the thought. That couldn't be it because she'd come back and become a guard.

"Molly told me she was with child," he said. "And that she wanted to raise the baby in the States."

I did my best not to react, but I had to ask, "Did she bring the baby back to Ireland with her?"

Seamus shook his head. "She lost the baby after we got there."

"And then you told her she needed to get a job," I said, the pieces clicking together.

"I didn't know what to do," he said. "I was young and dumb. I'd turned me back on me family after all they'd done. If me mam would have known I'd tried to take a grandchild from her, she'd be furious. And Molly and I were poor. You know what summies get paid now. It was even less when I started. But that's what Molly wanted."

The gruff man dropped off the beer, interrupting the story.

"I'm so sorry," I said, squeezing his hand in mine.

"It's me who should apologize," he said. "I should have told you all of this a long time ago. But everything was so good with us, I didn't want to muck it up."

"It's okay," I said. "I'm not angry. I'm just so sorry you had to go through all that."

"If I'm bein' honest," Seamus said. "I was thinking about moving back right before I met you. But the minute I saw you, I knew you were my home. Even if that meant staying in the States."

My eyes filled up with tears.

Seamus let go of my hand. "I wasn't going to do this here. It's really the worst place for this sort of thing." He was reaching into his pocket again.

I sucked in a breath and glanced around. No one was going to interrupt this time.

I smiled and sat up straighter.

He slid from the booth and bent down on his knee.

The box was in his hand.

He opened it to reveal a gorgeous oval diamond surrounded by tiny emeralds set on a thin pavé band.

"Will you marry me, Shayla?"

I slipped out of the booth and got down on the dirty floor with him. "It would be an honor to marry you. And to live our lives here, in Ireland."

Seamus gathered me up in his arms and hugged me tightly. "I love you so much."

"I love you too."

He let me go and, with shaky hands, slid the ring onto my finger.

"It's perfect," I said.

"You're perfect." He cupped my face in his hands and kissed me.

"Congratulations," a gruff voice said. "Here's your burgers."

We stood and returned to our seats as the man placed our meals in front of us. "Don't think you'll be getting a free meal just because you got engaged."

He didn't wait for a reply before walking back to the bar.

"I'm sorry," Seamus said.

I laughed. "It's okay. This is perfect. Absolutely perfect."

31

The burger was greasy but delicious. With every bite I took, I couldn't help but admire the ring on my hand.

"I helped design it," Seamus said when he caught me looking at it for probably the thousandth time. "Do you like it?"

"I love it," I said. "It's gorgeous. But it must have cost you a fortune."

"It did," he said. "I guess it's a good thing we'll be coming into some inheritance because that was my entire savings."

We.

He said we'd be coming into an inheritance. Because we would be married. My heart warmed at the thought of being able to give my kids all the things my mother couldn't afford to give me.

"Where will we live?" I asked.

"Probably with Mam and Da until we can find a place for ourselves," he said. "If you'd like, we can move to Dublin. It's much bigger than Ballywick and has more of the amenities you're used to in Prairie City."

Prairie City sounded so American compared to Ballywick. It would take some time for me to get used to the fact that I was moving to Ireland.

"I think we should stay here," I said. "Close to family."

Seamus smiled. "I hoped you'd say that."

"Well, well, well, if it isn't the lovebirds," Killian said, walking up to our booth with Nuala and her mother, Rose, in tow. "I'm surprised I didn't find you wearing the faces off each other again."

"And I'm surprised to see you here at all," Seamus said.

"Shove over." Killian pushed his way into the booth next to Seamus. "Go on, sit by Shayla." He motioned for Nuala and her mother to sit.

I moved toward the wall, giving them room.

"I thought you were going back to Dublin," Seamus said. "To change the locks."

I glanced over just in time to see Nuala roll her eyes.

"We made up," Killian said.

It was at this point I realized he was slurring his words.

"He proposed for real this time," Nuala said. "We'll get a ring when the inheritance comes through."

I slid my left hand to my lap, but not quickly enough.

"Bring that back up here," Killian practically shouted, reaching for my hand.

"Killian," Seamus warned.

I brought my hand back on top of the table. Nuala and her mother gasped at the sight of the ring.

"Yeh finally did it, eh?" Killian said, slapping his cousin on the back.

Seamus smiled. "I shoulda done it a long time ago."

"Just please don't tell me yeh did it here in this shite hole." Killian looked around with disgust all over his face.

"What's wrong with this place?" Rose asked.

"The burgers are greasy, the beer is stale, and it smells

like someone took a piss on the floor." Killian at least had enough common sense through his drunken haze to keep his voice down.

"Don't let Larry hear you say that," Nuala said. "He'll turn yeh out faster than a feral cat."

Killian didn't look worried about it.

It amazed me the difference between the two men. They'd both grown up with an unlimited amount of money at their disposal, on the same property, only with different parents. How they could be so polar opposite was beyond me. Maybe America had done Seamus some good. Or maybe he'd always been this way.

"What can I get yeh?" Larry asked in his gruff voice.

"Three pints and three burgers," Killian said.

Neither of the women next to me objected. Maybe this place only had Guinness and burgers.

"I hear they'll be making an arrest in yer uncle's case soon," Larry said. "Tis too bad he died. He sure did make for some good fodder."

"An arrest?" I asked. "Where did you hear that?"

Was that why Molly had to leave so quickly?

Larry smirked at me. "That's cute." He walked away without answering my question.

"This is the place people come to stay anonymous, remember?" Seamus said.

I smiled, but something wasn't settling right in my stomach. Maybe it was just the greasy burger. "Rose, you knew Alabaster pretty well, didn't you?"

"He's the reason for my parents' divorce," Nuala said, bitterness seeping through her every word.

"Nuala," her mother chided her.

"How so?" I asked, not caring that Rose didn't want to talk about it.

"My father found them sleeping together," Nuala said.

"They'd been having an affair for years. My father made me get a DNA test to make sure I wasn't Alabaster's child."

"That definitely would have changed things," Killian said. "Can you imagine being our cousin all this time after Seamus and I had both—"

"Killian, stop," Seamus said. "That's a disgusting thought."

"And, yet, if I had been Alabaster's child, I'd be in a much different position right now, wouldn't I?" Nuala said.

"You'll get your hands on his money," Killian said, reaching across the table for her hand. "Even if it's because you'll be marrying his nephew."

She let him hold her hand, but I couldn't help but notice she didn't clench his fingers with hers. How could he not see she was just in it for the money?

Or maybe he could and didn't care. Which was even worse in some ways.

"Did you know mistletoe is poisonous?" I asked.

"I didn't," Nuala said, then turned to her mom. "Did you?"

"Of course, I did," Rose said. "I'm a florist. But it's not as poisonous as people have made it seem."

"Is that right?" I asked, feigning interest.

"It might make someone feel sick to their stomach, but it likely won't kill them," Rose said.

Larry dropped off three pints without so much as a word to any of us.

"Did yeh try to poison Alabaster?" Seamus asked, not sticking with my more subtle approach.

"That's just grand," she said. "Just because I know a thing or two about mistletoe poisoning, you're gonna go on and blame me for his death?"

"Oh, she didn't kill him," Killian said. "I was there when they were arguing."

"What do you mean you were there?" Rose said.

"I was hiding," he said. "Uncle told me to go out through the bathroom, but I didn't. I wanted to see what the two of you were up to."

I gaped at Killian.

"Killian, you need to keep your mouth shut right now," Nuala said, glancing over at Seamus, then me, then back to Killian. "Not another word, you hear me?"

32

"It was nothing bad," Killian said, not heeding his fiancée's warning. "She wanted him back, and he said no. Actually, he said you only lobbed the gob once."

Nuala looked over at her mother. "But I thought Da caught the two of you together?"

"That's what your da wanted you to think," Rose said. "He wanted you to think he left me because of it, but I left him. Alabaster and I were in love."

"That's not what it sounded like to me," Killian said. "He even said he was in love with someone else and had been for ages."

"Killian, that's enough," Nuala said, realizing how badly her drunk fiancé was incriminating her mother.

"It's okay," Killian said. "She only threw the vases. She didn't kill him."

Rose stood. "There's no reason for me to be defending myself. Alabaster flirted with me endlessly, led me on, and then turned me down. Course I was upset, but Killian's right, I didn't kill him. Maybe I put a little poison in his drink when he was on the ground. It wasn't enough to kill him. Just enough to make him regret messing with me."

Nuala gasped.

"That's enough of a confession for an arrest," Molly said, coming around the corner of the booths.

Rose gaped at her. "But I didn't kill him. I swear, I didn't."

Molly didn't reply to Rose but turned to us and said, "Thanks for your help. Especially you, Killian. We'll need a formal statement of everything you heard in the room that night."

"Okay," Killian said. "But it's not what you think. She only threw the vases. And maybe dropped some poison in his glass—though I didn't see her do that, so I wouldn't know."

"Will you just shut up?" Nuala screamed at him. "You have already ruined my mother's life." She stood and followed Molly and Rose out, pleading for Molly to let her mother go.

Killian stood and dropped a two hundred euro note on the table. "That should pay for our food." He turned and followed Nuala, shouting, "Come on, NuNu, I didn't mean it. I'm plastered."

I gaped at Seamus across the table. "Did that really just happen?"

"Do yeh think she did it?" Seamus asked.

I considered it for a moment. She admitted to poisoning his drink. But something wasn't sitting right. "If he died by poisoning, then I suppose perhaps she did. I don't understand why she would put the mistletoe on his lips, though, being a florist and all. Don't you think that would completely give her away?"

"It sounds like the perfect signature if she planned on becoming a serial killer," Seamus said.

"But maybe too obvious?" I shrugged. "I don't know. I'm

sure Molly knows what she's doing. I doubt she would have arrested Rose if she didn't have good reason."

Seamus didn't look so convinced. Even though I knew he loved me and wanted to marry me, I could still see the hurt, or maybe anger, in his eyes when Molly was the subject.

Larry dropped three burgers on the table and snatched up the two hundred euro note. "Tell that Garda ex of yours to stay the hell out of me place. And thank Killian for the tip."

"Shall we take these extra burgers up to the pub? See if anyone's hungry?" Seamus asked as he led us out of the restaurant, holding several to-go boxes.

"Won't Harry mind?" I asked.

"Prolly won't even notice," Seamus said. "At this point, the pub is likely filled to the brim. Plus, he stops servin' food at five."

I glanced at my phone screen. It was nine o'clock. And I had a text from Rylie.

"How's she doing?" Seamus asked.

"As good as you would expect."

"She's gonna be lost without ya."

"She'll be all right. She has her family and more friends than I can count."

I opened my text message to see what she'd said.

SO . . . . . . ?

I laughed. "Do you mind if I tell her?" I showed him her message.

"She knew?"

I shook my head. "I think everyone knew."

"Did you?"

"I hoped." I shrugged.

He smiled. "Go ahead, but tell her to keep it quiet until we can tell our parents."

I took a picture of the ring as we went through the door and hit send.

She replied within milliseconds.

IT'S GORGEOUS!

Another message followed closely behind.

Why are there police lights in the background?

33

I looked up to see what Rylie was talking about and found Seamus staring at the scene before us.

Sure enough, a whole gaggle of Gardaí cars with flashing lights surrounded the flower shop next door.

"They must have found some evidence in Rose's shop," Seamus said.

We walked through to get to Seamus' car and watched as Molly loaded Rose into the back of the Gardaí car. Killian stood next to Nuala, begging her for forgiveness as she just stared, teary-eyed, at her mother.

"We'll catch up with them later," Seamus said. "Let's not let these burgers get cold."

As we drove to the pub, my emotions ranged from excitement every time I caught a glimpse of the ring to unease when I thought about Rose being arrested.

Had Molly actually found something? Or was she just arresting the most obvious suspect?

The bar was packed like Seamus said it would be. We walked in with the burgers and were nearly attacked by hungry people.

"Hey, not for you," Seamus said to a man wearing a dark green sweater. "After what yeh did to me cousin, yer not welcome to me food."

"I didn't do nothing to yer cousin," the man shouted.

Then it clicked. This must be Chadwick.

"Then why does she have bruises on her wrists?" I said. "We know you hurt her the other night."

He looked me up and down, then glanced at the woman who had appeared at his side.

"Did yeh say Chadwick was with another woman the other night?" she asked.

"I did," I said.

She glared up at him. "Yeh said you were done with her. Why'd yeh give me this God-forsaken ring if yeh were just gonna go back to that little social media whore?"

He grabbed her by the arm and started to drag her out of the bar.

I stepped in front of them. "I won't let you hurt this woman like you did Aoife. Let her go. If she doesn't want to be with you now that she knows who you truly are, that's her prerogative."

Chadwick gaped at me. Then his face turned to anger. He bent down so his nose was inches from mine.

Little did he know I was a police officer who'd had her fair share of men in my life trying to intimidate me. I wasn't backing down.

"I didn't cheat on me girlfriend—fiancée—Aoife is a lying sack of—"

He didn't get to finish his statement before he went down like a ton of bricks with Seamus staring at him from above.

His fiancée ran out of the pub.

"Don't you ever come near me family or me girl again," Seamus said.

Chadwick hurried back to his feet and looked as if he might punch Seamus.

But Harry stepped between them. "Get outta here, Chadwick."

"But he pushed me," Chadwick complained.

"Yeh was in his girl's face. What do yeh expect?" Harry asked. "Maybe if yeh knew how to treat a lady, yeh wouldn't be in this predicament. Now, out yeh go."

Chadwick did, reluctantly.

"Do the two of yeh want Aoife's booth?" Harry asked once Chadwick was gone. "She just called and said she wouldn't be needing it tonight. Probably found out that tosser was here."

"Sure," Seamus said.

Harry walked us over to a booth in the corner where some of the sound died. It didn't have the same acoustics as the one in the center of the pub, but it was nice not being right in the thick of everything.

"Can I get yeh some of the black stuff?" Harry asked when we were seated.

"First, you can answer a question for me," Seamus said. "Do you have a minute to sit?"

He looked back at his rowdy pub.

"I insist," Seamus said in a serious and confident tone I'd never heard him use before.

Harry glanced at me and then at Seamus and obliged. "But only for a minute. Me staff needs the help tonight. And don't be thinking I didn't see yeh bring that trash in from Larry's."

"What's it matter? It's not like yer servin' food right now." Seamus turned to me. "Larry and Harry are brothers."

"Before yeh ask, me sisters' names are Sharry and Carry. Not spelled like normal, spelled like Harry with an a-r-r-y at the end." Harry looked irritated by this. "Now, what yeh be needin' to ask me?"

"Why'd you throw that brick through me parents' window?" Seamus asked.

"I woulda thought the note explained it quite nicely," Harry said.

"We weren't allowed to read the note," I said. "It's part of the crime scene."

"Yeh didn't get to the note before that tosser kicked the bucket?" Harry shook his head.

"Yeh hit him in his dead head," Seamus said. "Didn't yeh see him in there?"

"Sure I did. With her." He pointed at me. "Right before I threw the brick."

I shook my head. "I wasn't in the office with Alabaster when the brick went through the window."

"Well, no," he said. "I said right before I threw the brick. He wasn't in the office when I threw it. At least, I didn't think he was. I couldn't see the floor. Shite. Are yeh sayin' I hit a dead guy with a brick?"

"Why'd you duck right before you threw the brick?" I asked.

"Because I saw yeh running away from the side of the house. I didn't want yeh to see me there before I got my message across."

Seamus looked at me, not necessarily accusingly, but maybe questioningly.

"It wasn't me," I said. "I heard the brick go through the window from inside the house. I was the first one there, remember? If I was running away from the house, how would I have gotten back so quickly?"

Harry shrugged.

"I know you didn't kill him," Seamus said. "Is there any

way you could describe what the woman was wearing in the room with my uncle before you ducked?"

"Blue? Maybe Black? Couldn't tell ya for sure," he said. "I was too angry."

"What was the message? Why were you angry?" Seamus asked.

"That lying, cheating, no-good uncle of yours owes me money," Harry said. "He's been hiding behind yer mam long enough."

"Which uncle?" Seamus asked.

"Which uncle do yeh think?" Harry asked, then stood. "If I was aiming to off one of 'em, it wouldn't have been Alabaster."

He strode away, and I had a feeling we weren't going to get our beer anytime soon.

Seamus sat back in the booth and thought about this for a moment. "There were several guests who had long blonde hair at the party."

"Maybe Molly has the DNA test back from the hair we found in the passage," I said. "That would be a pretty clear indicator of who it was. Especially if Harry saw her in there with Alabaster right before he threw the brick."

"Do you think the hair DNA was from Rose, and that's why they arrested her?" Seamus said.

"Wasn't her hair up that evening?" I asked. "I suppose she could have let it down. Maybe she went in for a second round to convince Alabaster to be with her."

"Or maybe she went in to finish him off," Seamus said.

34

On our way home from the pub, after waiting over an hour in vain for our beer, I suggested we stop and check on Aoife.

"Why?" Seamus asked.

"I haven't seen much of her, and didn't Harry say she was supposed to be at the pub tonight?"

Seamus shrugged. "She's probably out with her friends somewhere else."

"If so, maybe Shannon will give me a tour of the castle. Before it's out of the family?"

"I forgot I hadn't shown you around the castle," Seamus said. "With everything going on, it slipped my mind."

A sound came over the car speakers, and Seamus pushed a button on the screen mounted in the dash.

"Hello?"

"It's me," Gráinne's voice blared.

Seamus nearly swerved off the road.

"Hello?" she said. "Are you there?"

Seamus righted the car, then reached to turn the volume down.

"We're here," Seamus said. "The volume was up so it sounded like you were yelling."

"I wasn't yelling," Gráinne said.

"I know that, Mam. It just sounded like it."

"Well, I wasn't. I'm perfectly grand. I just wanted to check in and see if you had fun in town."

Seamus glanced over at me and smiled. "She said yes."

Gráinne squealed, making me thankful the volume wasn't still up. It might have blown the speakers. "That's wonderful. Donal?" Her voice got quieter as she called for her husband. "Shayla said yes. He finally proposed!"

"If that's all," Seamus said. "We're going to see if Aoife or Shannon will give us a tour of the castle."

"That's fine, just fine," she said. "I'll get all the details later. Congratulations! I'm so happy you'll be joining the family, Shayla!"

"Me too," I said, a huge smile on my face. "Thank you!"

"We love you, kids," Gráinne said.

"Love you too, Mam," Seamus said, then pressed the call end button. "Do you think we should give your mam a ring before we tour the castle? Just so she knows around the same time as we told my parents?"

Why I was dreading this conversation was beyond me. Mom liked Seamus well enough. The handful of times they'd been around each other, they'd gotten along.

It was probably because I would be moving to Ireland, and I didn't want her to be disappointed in that decision. Not telling her, though, just because I was worried about her reaction wasn't terribly fair.

"Sure, let's call her."

The phone rang a few times and then she answered. "Gooday, mate." I could hear the alcohol in her voice.

"We're in Ireland, mom, not Australia," I said, trying to keep my voice light.

She giggled on the other end.

"I just wanted to give you some news," I said. "Exciting news."

"I have exciting news too," Mom said, carefully enunciating her words like she always did when she'd had too many to drink.

"Oh?" I asked.

"I'm engaged," she said.

All the air deflated out of my lungs. Of course, she was.

"When did that happen?" I asked.

"The proper way to respond to an engagement announcement is congratulations, Shayla." She apparently wasn't too drunk to correct my manners.

"I'm sorry, congratulations," I said. "When did that happen?"

"Tonight," she said.

Seamus reached across the center console and squeezed my hand.

I felt like I wanted to cry.

"And you should see the ring. It's at least two karats."

I glanced down at my own probably ten to fifteen karat ring. "That's great, Mom. Now, can I tell you my news?"

"Let me guess—you're quitting the police department and moving to Ireland?" She snickered, and I could hear other people laughing in the background.

I could just imagine her rolling her eyes, thinking I was quitting because I couldn't cut it.

"Actually, yes," I said. "Oh, and I got engaged tonight too."

"You can't be serious about moving to Ireland," Mom said. "I was only joking. Though not about quitting the department. I figured that was coming after the stories I'd heard from some of the guys."

I sucked in a breath and said, "The proper way to respond

to an engagement announcement is congratulations. I love you, Mom. Bye."

I hung up the phone before she could respond, knowing full well she wouldn't call back to apologize for what she'd said.

"I'm really sorry about your mam," Seamus said.

I wiped the tears from my cheeks. "It's the way she's always been. I guess I just figured she'd be happy for me. Or sad that I was moving. Or angry, even. Not—" I waved my hands in the air. "—whatever that was."

"She sounded like she was tipsy," Seamus said, trying to smooth things over. "I'm sure everything will be different tomorrow."

The thing about having great parents is that you can't even fathom ones that aren't great. I knew deep down things would not be different in the morning. But I didn't have the heart to tell him that.

"Let's go check on Aoife," I said, opening the door of the car.

Seamus held my hand up the stairs, looking at me every once in a while as if I might break into tears again.

"Aoife's not here," Shannon said when she opened the door. "Out with friends."

"Ah, we wondered," Seamus said. "I know it's late, but would yeh mind giving Shayla the tour?"

Shannon's face brightened. "I'd love to. It may be the last time I get to do so. The new owners take possession directly after Christmas. At least they let us spend one last Christmas here."

"I suppose next year we could do it at me parents' house," Seamus said.

"I suppose we'll have to," Shannon said, letting in through the massive double doors to the grey stone castle. "Won't be enough room in the guesthouse, now will there?"

"I'm so sorry about how things have gone, Aunt Shannon. I wish it was different."

"I knew he was a gambler when I married him," she replied. "I just never thought it'd get this bad. Don't get me wrong. I'm thankful for everything your mam and da's done for us. I'll just miss this place."

As I looked around, I could see why. Though it wasn't as cozy as Gráinne and Donal's, it was still beautiful inside.

The walls were made of the original stone, but the floors were a shiny dark hardwood. Christmas lights hung around every door frame and wrapped the massive wooden beams on the high ceilings.

"This is amazing," I said.

"It's the nicest castle in Ireland," Shannon said, wiping a tear from her eye. "Aoife always said it'd be a great place for a B&B. I have to agree."

"The walls are original stone, but the wooden beams have been replaced and the stone floors covered in real hardwood." Shannon went into a complete history of the castle as we wove our way around the main level and then up the tight spiral stone staircase to the second floor. "Up here are the bedrooms."

She stopped at the first door in the long hall. "This is Aoife's room. I'm sure she won't mind you seeing it. She's done nothing but talk about how amazing you are since you got here. She rarely takes to people so easily."

"Shayla has a way with people and animals," Seamus said, pride in his voice. "You should have seen her with the horses. They all adored her."

"That's quite a compliment," Shannon said. "Those horses are temperamental beasts. I never did understand them."

Aoife's room didn't look like it was in a castle. It had been completely renovated to be modern while still having stone walls.

"Aoife is quite the interior designer," I said.

"Aoife is many things," Shannon said. "She can accomplish nearly anything she sets her mind to."

"When she was Miss Ireland," Seamus said. "She wanted to do video game programming as her talent. But settled for a standup comedy routine."

"I don't know which sounds harder, programming or comedy." The room was messy in an I-was-in-a-rush-to-leave sort of way. The bed was made with throw pillows piled high. The vanity was covered with expensive makeup products, and the nightstand held more books than a person could read— all of them classics. "Does Aoife read these?"

"She loves reading," Shannon said. "Though don't tell anyone that. She hates being pegged as smart. Beautiful? Funny? Charming? Yes. But if I dare mention a word about her academic achievements to her friends, she'll practically lose her mind."

"It's probably because Killian and I used to get into so many arguments over who was smarter between the two of us," Seamus said. "The whole while, she was probably smarter than the two of us put together."

"And two years younger," Shannon said, pride in her voice.

"Do you think I could peek in the closet?" I asked. I loved rich people's closets. There was something magical about them. And one in a castle? I was lightheaded at the mere thought.

"Oh sure," Shannon said. "Aoife won't mind a bit.

As I opened the closet, tiny lights lit from the door back to the full-length tri-fold mirrors in the back. Eventually, the entire space was illuminated by what I suspected was the most flattering light money could buy.

The smell of potent perfume and something else I couldn't quite put my finger on made my eyes water. "Whoa, she likes her fragrances."

Shannon stepped in and flipped on a switch. "I've asked her to ventilate it every once in a while, but she doesn't much listen to me."

On one side were rows and rows of shoes, jewelry, handbags, and hair accessories. There were even a few brightly colored wigs.

The other side was for the clothes, but the racks weren't packed. Each hanger had at least two to three finger widths between giving the clothes space to breathe. Beneath the hangers were rows of dressers. I could only imagine what was inside.

A long white tufted bench ran down the center covered with a few outfits that hadn't been replaced, probably after Aoife had tried them on. I picked up a pair of black pleather pants with a heart logo on the waistband and held them up. "These are super cute."

Shannon glanced at what I was holding and started cracking up. "I call those the duck pants because every time she takes a step in them, they squawk." She laughed harder, making Seamus and I chuckle too. "But a friend of hers is the designer, so she wasn't too thrilled I was acting the maggot about her friend's clothes."

I put the pants back down.

"Do you want to see the rest of the house?" Shannon asked.

I didn't have the guts to tell her that what I really wanted to do was stay in Aoife's room forever. It was like heaven, minus the smell.

She showed us a couple of spare rooms down the hallway —one was currently being used to wrap Christmas gifts. Shannon quickly closed the door before we could see much more than some wrapping paper and ribbon. "Nothing to see," she said. "I forgot Aoife had set up the wrapping station in there. She's very particular about how things are wrapped."

"She's always wrapped the presents," Seamus said. "Even when the staff offered, she'd turn them down."

"She says it's like meditation for her," Seamus said. "And it's a good thing we didn't rely on the staff all these years since we no longer have any."

You wouldn't be able to tell by how tidy everything was.

"I'm sorry to bring it up," Seamus said.

"It's no bother," Shannon said, plastering a smile on her face. "Don't think about it another second. Let's head back downstairs. I've saved the best for last."

I looked at Seamus eagerly. He smiled and nodded back at me. I didn't know what could be better than Aoife's bedroom, but I was excited to find out.

As we started down a different staircase—a much bigger one this time—we heard glass shattering from the main level.

"What was that?" Seamus asked.

Shannon didn't answer but tore off, running down the stairs.

35

Shannon took a turn in the direction opposite the front door, running incredibly fast for a woman her age and stature.

"Please no," she said to herself. "Not the Christmas room."

I recalled seeing a Christmas tree lit up through a gorgeous window that faced the front of the house.

It was probably the room she was about to show me. And the room that was currently on fire.

As we charged through the doorway, what was probably one of the most gorgeous spaces I'd ever been in was now engulfed in rapidly spreading flames.

Seamus tried to pull me out of the room, but I had to grab something first.

Shannon was calling the fire department as I slipped inside the room and picked up a brick with a note tied to it.

"Shayla, get out of there," Seamus called.

I happily heeded his request and ran back out of the room. He and Shannon led the way back through the house.

"What's going on?" Aoife asked with a yawn and a

stretch as she met us in the hall by the front door. She had on silky pink pajamas, pink lipstick, and matching fuzzy slippers.

"When did you get home?" Shannon asked.

"Home?" Aoife looked at her mother questioningly. "I've been home all evening. What's going on? Is something burning?"

"The Christmas room is on fire," Seamus said. "If the fire brigade doesn't get here soon, the whole place will go up in flames."

"On fire?" Aoife's face paled to a ghostly white. "How? What happened?"

"We can talk about that outside," Seamus said.

"But the castle is made of stone," Shannon said. "Surely it'll stay contained to that room."

"The floor is wood. The door is wood. The beams in the ceiling are wood," Aoife said, glancing up the staircase we'd just come down. "My things."

She darted off upstairs before anyone could stop her.

I didn't wait for permission. I ran after her.

Seamus was hot on my heels.

"They're just things," Shannon said. "Everything of real value has been sold."

Aoife wasn't listening. She threw open her bedroom door. I expected her to go for the jewelry, or the clothes, or maybe a photo album or computer.

Instead, she went straight to the books on the nightstand.

"I can help," I said. "What else do you need?"

She looked around the room. "Everything else is insured." Then her eyes widened. "The Christmas presents."

She shoved the books in my arms and ran off down the hall. I juggled the books and the brick I was still holding.

Seamus ran after her, but the fire was spreading from the first floor to the second.

The room she'd set up as the wrapping room was directly above the Christmas room.

She reached for the door handle but pulled her hand back and shook it.

Seamus grabbed her around the waist as she reached out again. "It's too late. If you open that door, we'll not make it out alive."

Aoife didn't seem to hear him. She struggled to get to the room, screaming, "The presents. It's our last real Christmas. The presents can't be ruined. I worked so hard."

Seamus turned her around to face him. "Stop. We have to leave."

She tried to turn back around, but he heaved her over his shoulder in one fluid motion.

"Go, Shayla," he said. "Get out of the house."

I turned and ran down the spiral staircase as smoke billowed up it.

I tried not to inhale too deeply and held onto Aoife's books for dear life. She was already losing her castle—her childhood home—and her last real Christmas. I couldn't let her lose her books, too.

The smoke was so thick by the time we reached the ground level, I couldn't see where I was going.

"Follow me," Seamus said, passing by me. "Hold on to my shoulder and try not to breathe."

I let him lead me out the front door. Once we were down the front steps and out of harm's way, Seamus asked Aoife, "If I put you down, will you run back inside?"

Aoife shook her head as her bright orange braid hung down so far it almost touched the ground.

Seamus put her back on her feet. She turned to look at the castle through teary eyes.

"How did this happen?" Seamus asked.

"Someone threw this through the window," I said,

pointing to where flames shot out of the front window. "I'm guessing it hit something that eventually started the fire."

"The candles," Shannon said. "I lit some candles in there tonight when I was reading."

Aoife gaped at her mother.

Sirens howled in the distance.

"They might as well turn around," Aoife said. "Everything is ruined."

36

It took the fire department hours to get the fire extinguished.

By the time the castle was nothing more than the original stone, the entire town was there to watch.

Aoife refused to go up to Gráinne's house, even though Shannon had. So Seamus and I stayed with her in his car with the heater turned on.

The brick I'd grabbed had a note tied on by a single strand of ribbon. It wasn't a red brick this time, but white instead. I probably wouldn't have read the message—it being evidence and all—but it was easy to see by the way it was tied.

You're next.

I'd handed it over to Molly the second she arrived.

By about six in the morning, I realized I was still holding Aoife's books in my lap.

I glanced in the backseat. Aoife was fast asleep, mascara smeared all over her face and her nose red from blowing it so many times. The thought of all she was losing broke my heart. It wasn't her fault her parents were bad with money. She deserved to have Christmas in her childhood home—or castle.

And it wasn't my fault my mother was incapable of kindness at times. I deserved to be happy, even if my mother couldn't be happy for me.

I glanced down at the ring on my finger and looked at a snoring Seamus. He was my family. My future. Sure, my mother would always be my mother, but I couldn't let her aloofness hurt my feelings. Not anymore. I had to stop giving her the power over my feelings.

The book on top of the stack was Dracula by Bram Stoker. I suspected it was a first edition by the wear on the cover and the spine.

I carefully opened it to find that it was worth far more than a mere first edition copy of Dracula. Between several of the pages were individual five hundred-euro notes.

As I turned the pages of the second book, more cash appeared.

No wonder Aoife wanted to grab them. They were worth a fortune.

The last book—and the largest—wasn't a book at all. It looked like a book but was actually a hardcover laptop case. I unzipped it as quietly as I could and peeked inside. There was a smartphone, more cash, an Irish passport, and several pieces of diamond jewelry.

"I guess you discovered my secret," Aoife whispered from behind me.

I was so startled, I nearly threw the books. "I-I wasn't. I didn't mean to. I'm sorry."

Aoife held her hand out for me to hand her the books. "It's fine. I trust you. But please keep it our secret." She glanced at Seamus. "Even from him."

I nodded. I felt horrible for going through her personal items. "I'm really sorry. I had no right."

"It's fine," Aoife said, looking out the window at the charred remains of her house. "Do you think they'll let me go inside now?"

The firefighters were rolling up their hoses and packing up their tools.

"It's probably not structurally sound," I said. "What do you need to get?"

"Nothing," she said, wiping her nose on the sleeve of the jacket Seamus had in the trunk—or boot, as he would call it —of his car. "It's nothing."

"Come on," I said. "Let's go ask." I needed to make up for my snooping. She'd done nothing but be kind to me. Popular girls always shied away from me, but not Aoife. She'd wanted to be my friend from the get-go.

And how did I repay her? By going through her belongings. Maybe leaving the police department was a good thing. Maybe I'd be able to keep my mind from revolving around investigations.

She didn't move from the backseat, still clutching her books to her chest.

"Okay, I'll go ask," I said. "You stay here in the warmth."

Only one of the fire trucks remained, and it looked more like a supervisor's vehicle than an actual fire truck. On the side, it said: Fire Investigation Unit.

Molly's Gardaí car was also still there, but no one was in sight.

I kept a large distance between myself and the charred castle as I circled around to the back. When I came to one side, Molly and a man who looked like he was in his late sixties squatted next to a white brick wall.

"I'm guessing that's where the brick came from," I said.

The man glanced at Molly, who nodded as if to say it was okay to speak to me.

"We also found some clothing, a cigarette butt, and a spool of the same ribbon as was affixed to the brick," the man said, holding up the evidence in his hands.

"You can't possibly think it was Harry this time," I said. "There's no way he'd fit in those clothes. And the cigarette butt has lipstick on it."

"This time?" Molly asked.

Shoot.

I hadn't told her my theory about it being Harry yet.

"Harry told us last night," I said. "I hadn't gotten around to mentioning it."

"What exactly did he tell you?" Molly asked.

"He said he threw the brick into the window. He saw someone who looked like me in the study with Alabaster, then he saw the same person running away from the house, so he ducked down. When he stood back up, the den was empty, so he threw the brick. He didn't know Alabaster was in the room already."

Molly stood up slowly, her face angry. "Why didn't you tell me this sooner?" Her eyes flashed to the ring on my finger. "Ah, seems you had more important things to be worryin' about."

"I was going to tell you," I said, not letting her goad me about my engagement. "But it was late."

"What happens if he's missing? You might have let a murderer get away."

"Murderer?" I asked.

"And arsonist," the man added.

"This wasn't arson," I said. "He threw a brick, and it hit a candle. Arson is deliberately setting fire to something."

"Destruction of property then," the man said.

"Let's go back to the murder thing," I said. "I thought you arrested Rose for Alabaster's murder?"

"Alabaster didn't die of poisoning," Molly said. "The tox reports came back negative for anything other than alcohol. And the hair was synthetic, so no DNA."

"Then how did he die?" I asked.

"I'd venture to guess it was from a brick being chucked at his head." Molly pursed her lips. "You better hope Harry's still at the pub like he always is."

"Or what?" I asked. "I'm not a Garda."

"You're right, you're not," Molly said. "So stop trying to be one."

37

I stormed off back to the car, got into the passenger side, and slammed the door.

"Jaysus, Mary, and Joseph," Seamus shouted. "What the hell's the matter wit ya?"

I turned to see his groggy, yet startled, face. "I'm sorry. I didn't mean to wake you."

"Did they say we could go in?" Aoife asked.

I'd completely forgotten to ask. Shoot. "I forgot to ask them."

Aoife's face drooped. "It's okay."

"You want to go into the castle?" Seamus asked. "Why?"

"I want to see if there's anything left," Aoife said, not meeting his eye.

"I'd go back and ask, but I'm pretty sure Molly would deny just about all of my requests right now since she's blaming me for letting a murderer go." I crossed my arms over my chest like a child pouting.

Normally, I'd uncross them after hearing my mother's voice in my head telling me not to act so childishly. But I wouldn't listen to her voice in my head anymore.

Seamus rubbed his eyes. "My brain's a bit foggy. Can you explain what yeh mean about lettin' a murderer go? Did yeh somehow sneak out of the car last night, hitch a ride to town, and break Rose out of the clink?"

"Apparently, she's not the murderer. The toxicology report came back negative for poison."

"I'm still not following," Seamus said.

"They think Harry did it," I said. "They think the brick killed Alabaster."

"When it hit him in the head?" Seamus asked.

"And they figure he probably threw the brick last night too," I said.

"That's ridiculous," Aoife said, still looking out the window and clutching her books. "Harry wouldn't do something like that. Plus, he was at the pub all night."

"It doesn't add up," I said. "They're missing something."

"Maybe he choked on the mistletoe," Aoife said.

"It wasn't in his mouth," Seamus said. "It was across his lips."

"But that still doesn't explain how it got there if the brick hit him in the head from outside," I said. "Someone had to have put it there after the brick went through the window. And not Harry because he was running—limping—away."

"Who else has blonde hair?" Seamus asked.

"Blonde hair?" Aoife said. "Who said the person had blonde hair?"

"Harry," I said. "And it wasn't real hair. It was synthetic."

A knock at the window stopped our conversation.

I turned to see Molly staring at me.

I pushed the button to roll the glass down.

"Harry ran," Molly said. "I had a Garda go to the pub to find him and the staff said they hadn't seen him since last night."

"When last night?" Seamus asked.

"Early," Molly said.

"We saw him there pretty early," Seamus said.

"He could have left right after that," I admitted, though I still didn't think he had killed Alabaster. Not intentionally, anyway. "We were there at least an hour waiting for beer that never showed up."

"Pissed off Harry, did yeh?" Molly asked, her tone mocking.

"Can Aoife go into the house?" I asked, ignoring her. "She'd like to see if anything is salvageable."

"I might be able to make that happen if you can help me with something," Molly said, directing her answer at Seamus.

"What is it now?" Seamus asked.

"We need to see the camera footage from last night," Molly said.

"If you let Aoife go into the house, I'll let you see the footage," Seamus said.

"I have to go in with her," Molly said. "It's still an active crime scene."

"Why's that?" I asked.

"The fire investigator has to look into every reason the house might have burned. Especially under the . . . circumstances." Molly chose her words carefully.

"They think me parents burned it down to collect the insurance," Aoife said, her voice monotone. "It's okay. I'd think the same thing if I was them."

Seamus turned slowly to look at Aoife. "Yeh really shouldn't be sayin' that."

"Why not?" Aoife said, anger coming through the sadness. "Me parents only care about money. They'd do anything to get it. Have you checked to see if me father was at the party the night of Uncle Alabaster's murder?"

Molly didn't reply. Surely she had.

"I'd bet me entire inheritance that me father killed him

before I'd bet Harry did." Aoife's porcelain face was pink with fury. "He never cared about anyone but himself."

"Aoife, that's enough," Seamus said. "Go look through the house. Then we can get up to me parents'. I need a cup of coffee before we dive into more surveillance footage."

Aoife handed me the books. "Look after these while I'm gone."

I took that as a sign she'd forgiven me for going through them.

"Hold on," Molly said, glancing at her phone as Aoife got out of the car. She let out a frustrated groan.

"What?" I asked.

"Alabaster didn't die by the brick either," Molly said. "He died of suffocation."

I glanced at her with eyebrows raised.

"Fine, you were right," Molly said. "Harry's not the killer. But he still threw at least one brick, if not two."

"That puts us back at square one," Seamus said, frustration in his voice.

Molly put her phone back in her pocket and glanced at Aoife. "Ready?"

Aoife and Molly started toward the castle.

"Do you think Clara could have done it?" I asked Seamus gently. "She was the only other one who was in there with him that I know of."

"I dunno." Seamus shrugged. "Uncle Alabaster probably tried the whole mistletoe bit. He always did favor Clara, but to try and kiss her? It's disgusting. I'd probably want to kill him too."

"Mistletoe?" Something caught in my mind.

"Yeah," Seamus said. "He probably tried to kiss her as he did with you."

"Right," I said. "And that would be why she would have left the mistletoe on his mouth, to make a point."

"It just doesn't seem like Clara." Seamus shook his head.

"That's because it wasn't," I said. "Did you tell anyone about the mistletoe?"

"No, did you?"

"Who would I tell?" I asked.

"Dunno."

"And I'd bet my left leg Molly didn't tell anyone."

"But I like your left leg," Seamus said. "Bet your earlobe or something."

"I need my earlobes for earrings," I said.

"And for me to kiss." He leaned over and kissed my earlobe, sending shivers down my spine.

"Mmm, you know how much I love that," I said. "But we can't right now. I need to get inside. I think Molly is in trouble."

38

I left the books on the seat. "Don't let these out of your sight."

"Do you need me to come with you?" Seamus asked.

"I'll be okay," I said, then closed the door.

I raced up the steps, careful to take the path I'd seen Molly and Aoife take. The last thing I needed was this castle coming down on top of me.

Once inside—though inside was now basically outside without a roof—I listened for voices.

Mumbling came from the second floor.

How had I not seen it? The pink lipstick on the cigarette butt, the wigs, the designer sweatpants. And then the mistletoe.

She wouldn't have known about the mistletoe if she hadn't been there.

"Aoife, you don't want to do this," Molly said. "Put the gun down."

"I have everything I need to get me out of the country," Aoife said. "I was going to wait until after Christmas. One more Christmas in the castle with me family. Was that too much to ask after that slimy urchin of an uncle bought it out from under me?"

"Which uncle?" Molly asked. "Donal? Did Donal buy the castle?"

"Is Donal dead?" Aoife asked, her voice still in the same monotone.

"Yer tellin' me you killed Alabaster?"

Aoife just laughed. "Does it matter?"

"Course it does," Molly said. "Because in a few minutes, you're goin' to give me that gun, and I'll arrest you for murder."

"That's not how I see this happenin'."

Molly didn't reply.

"Don't you want to know me plan?"

"I have a feelin' you'll tell me whether or not I want to know," Molly said.

"Don't be mouthin' off to me," Aoife shouted. "I know where your little girl goes to school. Maybe after I take care of her mam, I'll pay her a visit too."

"Okay, I'm sorry," Molly said, her voice quivering. "Do what yeh will with me, but leave my child alone."

I peeked around the stone wall that used to be Aoife's bedroom, holding my breath. Thankfully, Aoife had her back to me. If Molly saw me, she didn't show it.

"That's more like it," Aoife said.

Molly's hands were tied behind her back. The room was in shambles other than what looked like a fire safe box with the lid opened.

"Depending on how this goes, you may or may not make it out of here alive." Aoife started pacing, waving the gun around as she talked.

I ducked back behind the wall. I needed to disarm her without getting either of us shot.

Aoife continued, "I need to make sure I can get out of the country before you send all your guards after me."

When I heard Aoife's voice quiet, and her footsteps move away from me, I peeked in again.

This time, Molly glanced at me and shook her head so slightly it was almost hard to determine if I was seeing things. Was she telling me not to attack Aoife? She shook her head one more time, slowly but in a bit bigger motion this time.

I ducked back behind the wall just as Aoife turned to pace my way.

"But how will I do that when the moment I leave, you'll go right out there and tell my spoiled brat cousin and his stupid little girlfriend—oh excuse me, fiancée—I bet that really irks you, doesn't it? That he came back, not to be with you, but to get engaged to a stupid American."

Anger pulsed through me. I thought we were friends.

"She lied for you," Molly said.

"So what?" Aoife said. "She was so desperate to be my friend. Every time I told her how much I liked her, she looked at me with her too-big-for-her-face eyes as if I was Mother Mary reincarnated."

"If it helps my case, I won't go out there and tell them anything. I'll let you get away as long as you leave my daughter out of this."

"Why don't we talk about that daughter of yours."

"We will not speak about my daughter!" Molly shouted, her voice echoing off the stone. "I told you to leave her out of this!"

Aoife laughed.

I glanced down to find a large piece of charred wood about five feet from me on the other side of the hall. If I could get to it, I might be able to hit Aoife over the head and untie Molly.

I peeked around the corner again to check that Aoife was pointed away from me before I stepped as quietly as I could to the other side of the hall.

The stones floors were now made of ash and the original stone that had been under the hardwood. Between the large stones and all the rubble from the fire, it was hard to maneuver without twisting an ankle. Eventually, I made it to the other side without making too much noise.

At least, I thought I had.

"Couldn't be left out, could we?" Aoife's voice said behind me.

I turned but felt a tug on my hair as Aoife pulled me from behind and threw me onto the floor at Molly's feet. Pain shot up through my knees down to my ankles.

"How long have you been listening?" Aoife asked as I looked up at her.

"Long enough," I said. "I guess we weren't friends after all."

"Boo-hoo." Aoife did the crying motion with her fists balled and the gun still in her hand.

It was a nine-millimeter semi-automatic, and from what I could see, the safety was on.

"Why did you come in here?" Molly asked.

"Because I knew she did it," I said.

Aoife laughed. "That's a bunch of malarkey, and you know it."

"Is it?" I asked. "You messed up, and you're going to pay for it."

"Am I?" Aoife stepped closer to me. "Who will make me pay? The fat American or the lying Irish wench?"

"Maybe one of us," I said. "Maybe both."

"If you're so smart, why don't you tell me how you knew," Aoife said.

"Where do I start?" I asked. "I think it was the mistletoe

that gave you away. No one would have told you about the mistletoe in—or rather, on—Alabaster's mouth. Only the killer and a handful of people—people who can keep their mouths shut—knew."

"There's not a lot of those types of people around here," Aoife said, turning her attention to Molly. "But Molly is one. You have lots of secrets, don't you?"

I needed to get her attention back on me. To get her to come closer so I could get the gun from her without her flipping the safety and shooting us.

"Don't you want to know what else?" I asked.

Aoife huffed. "Fine, go ahead."

"There were the wigs in your closet which would account for the synthetic hairs we found." I glanced over where her closet had been. "Also, I'd be willing to bet the clothes you left outside were designed by your friend. You know the one whose trademark is a little heart?"

Aoife shuffled from one foot to the other.

"Then there's the fact that you were wearing the same shade of bright pink lipstick that was found on the cigarette butt outside. I bet it has some DNA on it too."

"So what? I smoke outside my house. Is that a crime now?" Aoife's voice wasn't as confident as it normally was.

"Did I mention we saw Chadwick last night? Seamus almost beat him up, but he insisted he hadn't seen you in ages. Of course, his fiancée didn't believe him."

Aoife's jaw dropped when I said, fiancée.

"He chased her out of the pub, though. Those bruises on your wrists aren't from him, are they? They're from Alabaster's hands, trying to get you to stop smothering him with the pillow."

Her gaze darted to her wrists.

"You had twigs in your hair the night of the party, consistent with exiting through the secret passageway. And I'd venture to guess the video footage that Molly wanted to check hasn't quite been altered yet, has it? Besides all the cash you have stashed in those books, you have your father's missing tablet. The phone-sized one inside that fake book, right?"

She didn't have time to respond before I lunged.

I grabbed the barrel of the gun with one hand.

She shrieked with rage.

I twisted the barrel and grabbed the back of the gun with my other hand.

She tried to yank it away, but it was too late.

Within seconds, the tables had turned, and I had the power.

I flipped the safety off and pointed the gun at Aoife. "Get on the ground with your hands behind your head."

39

When I untied Molly, she hugged me for a solid minute before smoothing out her uniform and pointing a finger at me. "You lied to me about your alibi."

"I thought she was my friend," I said.

Aoife mumbled, "Idiot."

Molly yanked Aoife toward the stairs and said to me, "It's her loss. She would have been lucky to have a friend like you."

I smiled at Molly, then said, "The tablet and some additional evidence are in the car with Seamus."

"That's my money," Aoife said. "You can't confiscate it."

"I'm not interested in the money," Molly said. "But the tablet will definitely be something the judge will want to give me a warrant for."

Aoife looked at me. "Tell me mam I'm sorry. I didn't intend on ruinin' Christmas. I just wanted to scare me father with the brick."

Seamus got out of the car when he saw Aoife handcuffed.

"What's going on? What happened?"

"I'll explain everything when we get up to the house," I said. "That coffee sounds pretty good right now."

"Shayla?" Molly said.

I turned back to look at her. "Yeah?"

"Thanks for your help in there. Yer an excellent officer. America's lucky to have you."

Seamus almost said something, probably about me moving to Ireland, but I nudged him and shook my head.

"I'm glad you're okay," I said. "Now, go home and be with your little girl."

"Little girl?" Seamus asked, his face paling.

I didn't think about the fact that he might be upset knowing she'd moved on and had a child after they'd lost theirs.

Molly didn't turn back to explain.

I wrapped my arms around Seamus' waist. "Sorry, you had to find out about it like that."

"I guess I never thought to ask if she'd moved on," he said. "I didn't see a ring on her finger."

"People can have babies without being married," I said. "Or maybe she just doesn't wear her ring at work."

Seamus watched as she slid into the passenger seat of her Gardaí car and drove away.

Gráinne, Shannon, and Donal were gobsmacked by the news. Shannon even fainted when I told her Aoife had unintentionally started the fire.

"And," Seamus said as I was wrapping up the story, "did yeh know Molly had a baby?"

Gráinne shook her head. "That'd be news to me."

"She seemed pretty shocked Aoife knew," I said. "I can

imagine she probably wants to keep it quiet so as not to put her child at risk."

"I'm sure your mother did the same when you were a baby," Gráinne said. "When do I get to meet her? Was she absolutely thrilled about the engagement?"

Seamus squeezed my hand. "I'm sure you'll meet her at the wedding."

I smiled and nodded, unsure I'd be able to form a sentence without tearing up.

"You've had a big morning," Gráinne said. "With all the adrenaline and emotion, I'm sure you're tired. Why don't the two of you take a rest. The solicitor is coming later this afternoon to tell us about the will. And then Shannon and I will be doing some Christmas shopping to make up for the things we lost in the fire. Would you like to come with us, Shayla?"

I nodded. "I'd love that."

Gráinne stood and opened her arms. I practically fell into them.

She pet my hair as I squeezed her probably tighter than was necessary.

"I'm so glad you're joining the family. We already love yeh."

My voice caught in my throat. I managed to croak out. "I already love you guys too."

Seamus fell asleep nearly instantly, but no matter how tired I was, I just couldn't get my brain to turn off.

How had I misjudged Aoife so drastically? Was I that desperate to be liked by the popular girl? How old was I? Thirteen?

I groaned and pulled out my cell phone.

I sent Rylie a rundown of what had happened the night

before, and she gave me all sorts of affirmation about how stupid my mom was, how it was Aoife's loss to not be able to be my friend, and how Aoife was obviously a good actress to fool not only me but her entire family.

By the time we'd finished texting, it was time to go downstairs and meet with the solicitor.

Seamus and I sat side by side at the massive formal dining room table next to Killian, Nuala, Shannon, Donal, and Gráinne. On the other side sat a man who looked like he might be around eighty.

"Thank you for coming," Killian said. "I'm sorry my father can't be here. He's tending to some business in town."

"Come off it," Shannon said. "He's getting wasted at the pub."

"And where is Aoife?" the man asked in a squeaky voice.

"She won't be joining us," Gráinne said. "She's been arrested for Alabaster's murder."

Shannon sucked in a sharp breath.

"That changes some things," the man said, flipping through papers. "I suppose the guards took my interview into account?"

"What interview?" Seamus asked.

"I was on the phone that night with Alabaster when a woman came in," he said. "I couldn't hear much, but it sounded like they were arguing. Then glass shattered."

His statement wasn't much to go off, but Seamus said, "I'm sure it was very helpful that you told them."

The man seemed pleased with himself. "Right, let's get down to business."

Nuala looked like she might come out of her seat with excitement.

"I'll be reading the will in the manner it was written. However, Irish law states that if a recipient of the inheritance is found guilty of murdering Alabaster, they shall forfeit their rights to any inheritance, and their inheritance will be split amongst the other two recipients."

Gráinne nodded once. He seemed to be primarily speaking to her.

"In the matter of Alabaster's estate—the cash will be divided evenly between Seamus, Killian, and Aoife, provided they do not find her guilty of murdering her uncle."

Killian looked like he might shout for joy. He leaned over and kissed Nuala so passionately, I had to turn away. I glanced at Seamus, who simply smiled and shrugged.

"His cottage is willed to Seamus."

Seamus' head popped up to look at the man in surprise.

"The castle—which he recently acquired—was to be left to Aoife. Now that it's burned, there's a matter of the insurance money and the property. If Aoife is found guilty of murder, I assume the two of you gentlemen will be able to work out who gets what, correct?"

Killian looked at Nuala, who wrinkled her nose. He turned to Seamus. "You can have it."

"Are you certain?" the solicitor asked.

Killian shrugged. "We don't need a burned-down castle or the tiny bit of insurance money that will go with it."

The solicitor slid a piece of paper to Killian. "If you're certain, please sign here."

Killian signed without a second thought.

"For both Gráinne and Shannon, he left these." The solicitor pulled two large wooden boxes from beside him on the floor. "He asked that they not be opened in the presence of anyone else. Once they're open, you may do with the contents as you wish."

Gráinne and Shannon stared down at the boxes as if they were traps.

"For Donal, he left this." The solicitor handed Donal a set of what looked like car keys.

Donal smiled as he took the keys in his hands as gently as he would a baby bird fallen from the nest. He wiped a tear from his eye.

"With that, I'm finished," the solicitor said. "If you sign these documents, I'll give you each your shares of the money."

As Killian and Seamus signed their paperwork, Shannon asked, "What about Geoffrey?"

"Ah yes," the solicitor said. "I almost forgot. Alabaster left a simple message for Geoffrey that I was instructed to speak aloud to the family."

Seamus and Killian looked up mid-signatures.

"Geoffrey, you're a piece of shite, and you get nothing." He put the piece of paper with the note in front of Shannon. "You may give it to Geoffrey when you see him next."

Shannon started giggling. Then her laughter turned into sobs.

Gráinne patted her on the back and she leaned over and put her head on Gráinne's shoulder.

Killian pushed his paperwork back at the solicitor who, in turn, handed him an envelope.

As Killian was tearing his envelope open, dollar signs practically coming out of his eyes like in a cartoon, the solicitor handed Seamus his envelope.

Killian pulled out a check and did a double-take. "This can't be right. Is this some kind of joke?"

Seamus opened his and showed me.

The check was in the amount of fifty-thousand euros.

"What? What's wrong?" Nuala asked.

Killian tipped his envelope upside down as if money might magically fall out of it. "That can't be it. He was worth millions. Possibly billions. Fifty thousand is chump change."

"Ah yes," the solicitor said, a smile quirking up the

corners of his mouth for the first time. "Alabaster said there might be a slight bit of confusion."

"Please don't tell me he gave it all to a feline shelter," Killian said, turning his accusatory stare on Seamus.

Seamus laughed and shrugged.

"No," the solicitor said, a confused look coming over his face. "Just before he died, he ordered me to transfer most of his savings into an account for his daughter and grand-children."

"Daughter?" Killian asked. "Uncle Alabaster didn't have a daughter."

"Did you know he had a daughter?" Seamus asked his mom.

Gráinne smiled. "I suspected."

Shannon took her head off Gráinne's shoulder and studied her.

"Why don't you tell them, in case I'm mistaken," Gráinne said to the solicitor.

He nodded. "Alabaster has one daughter by the name of Clara Walsh."

"Clara?" Seamus asked.

"That's preposterous," Killian said. "Clara's nothing more than a servant's child."

"I'm the child of a servant and a billionaire," Clara said, stepping into the dining room. "And I'm your cousin."

40

S eamus stood and hugged Clara. "It's only right that you'd get the money."

"Right?" Killian said, standing to his feet. "There's nothing right about it. What did she ever do to deserve it?"

"What did you?" Magella asked, stepping into the room next to her daughter.

"Don't you dare speak to me that way," Killian said.

"Killian, shut up," Shannon said, standing. "You don't deserve a single cent of your uncle's money, do you hear me? Now, get out before I rip up that check, and you get nothing."

Killian grabbed the check off the table and ripped it up himself. "I don't want Uncle's ridiculous pocket change. Nuala and I don't need money to be happy."

"Speak for yourself," Nuala said. "I'm out."

She left the room as we all stared in disbelief.

"I told yeh to watch out for that one, but yeh wouldn't listen to me," Seamus said.

Killian threw his hands up in the air and sat back at the table.

"If yeh really don't want the inheritance, I'll need you to sign this document," the solicitor said.

Killian signed away his rights as Seamus and Clara spoke excitedly.

"How long have you known?" Seamus asked.

"That night, the night he died, when I was in the study with him, that's what we were discussing," she said, then turned to me. "I'm sorry I wasn't honest with you, but I hadn't quite come to terms with it myself."

"You were the love of his life," Seamus said to Magella.

"And he was the love of mine," she replied. She turned to Gráinne. "Thank you for keeping our secret all these years."

"It was my pleasure. I knew how happy you made each other," Gráinne said.

"I only wish we'd have had more time," Magella said. "After I gave him permission to tell Clara, I was certain we'd be a proper family. I should have done so long before now."

"Why didn't you?" I asked.

"I didn't want my Clara having everything handed to her," she said. "I've been around wealthy children my entire life, and I didn't want my own to be like them. No offense."

"None taken," Seamus said.

"Speak for yourself," Killian said, shoving the signed papers back at the solicitor. "I'm leaving. Have a nice life."

He walked out of the room, shortly followed by the solicitor.

"Why don't you take Shayla over to the cottage and show her around," Magella said to Seamus. "It'll be a nice place for the two of you to stay when you visit. Alabaster had strict orders for his staff on how to prepare the house for you once he died."

"Shall we?" Seamus said.

"Definitely," I said, excitement running through me. Little

did the people in the room know we would be making Ireland our permanent residence.

The sun was dropping in the sky as we made our way across the drive and away from Seamus' parents' house and the castle.

"Can you believe Killian gave everything up?" Seamus asked. "I mean, I know you don't really know him, but that was insane."

"Do you think he'll change his mind?"

"Not a chance," Seamus said. "Killian's a right stubborn one. Once he makes a decision, he won't veer from it."

"When should we tell your family we're moving to Ireland?"

"I thought it'd make for a good Christmas gift," Seamus said. "Especially since everything else burned down."

"What do you want for Christmas?" I asked. I'd already bought him a few small things, but I'd never actually asked him what he wanted.

"I already got what I wanted." He lifted my hand and spun me around. "I get to marry the woman of my dreams."

I giggled, then gasped.

The cottage was not at all what I expected.

It was far larger than any cottage I'd ever seen. Big windows contrasted the stone exterior. Each door and main level window was framed by what looked like rough concrete. Vines climbed the sides.

"This is the cottage?"

"We don't have to live here," Seamus said quickly. "Just because Uncle gave it to me doesn't mean it has to be our home."

I turned and looked at him. "It's gorgeous. I'd be honored to live here."

"Yeh haven't even seen the inside yet," Seamus laughed.

"Right," I said, training my face into a serious expression. "I must see the inside first."

Seamus laughed at my fake seriousness.

The pale green door had an envelope hanging outside. On the back of the envelope were two words—welcome home.

Seamus pulled the envelope from the door, opened the letter, and read.

"I've written no less than a hundred of these letters, and, yet, I wonder if this will be the one you receive. You see, you've returned home with a lovely young girl I suspect will be your wife. And if I die before the two of you move to Ireland, which I sincerely hope you do, I would be honored for you to raise your family in my cottage.

"Speaking of the cottage, everything inside is yours, Seamus. Don't let anyone tell you otherwise. And if you die once you're married, everything will belong to Shayla. Not your children. Not your family. Your wife.

"For I wish I'd done more to serve the love of my life and my daughter. I suspect you know by now that Clara is not merely Magella's daughter but mine as well. Please treat her well and make sure Aoife is kind to her. They got on fine when Clara was a servant's daughter, but I fear when the tables are turned, and Clara has more money than she knows what to do with, Aoife will take her jealousies out on Clara.

"Finally, before I go, I want to thank you for coming home. Even if you don't stay—which I wish you would—I know your mother and father were extremely pleased to have you." Seamus's voice caught in his throat. "I love you, Seamus, and am proud of you. Sincerely, Alabaster O'Malley."

I wiped tears from my cheeks.

Seamus did the same.

Neither of us said a word as he opened the door and led me into our new home.

Thank you so much for reading *Mistletoe Malarkey*!

If you'd like to read more about how Shayla and Seamus met, check out the Rylie Cooper Mystery Series starting with *Catfished*!

What do you think? Would you like Shayla to have her own series? Email me and let me know!

I'd love it if you'd take a moment to review this book on Amazon, Goodreads, or Bookbub.

I love hearing from my readers! Feel free to email me at stellabixbyauthor@gmail.com.

ACKNOWLEDGMENTS

Thank you to my awesome husband who jumped right on board when I mentioned traveling to Ireland several years ago. Since then, I've wanted to set a book in that beautiful country.

Thank you to Groupon and Great Value Vacations for offering such an awesome travel package. I can't wait to get back to Ireland soon!

Thank you to Carlene O'Connor for writing *Murder at an Irish Christmas*. I wish there were more cozies based in Ireland at Christmas!

Thank you to my readers, friends, family, and fellow authors. I can't believe this will be my sixteenth book published in less than four years. I couldn't do it without all of you!

Thank you, God. For literally everything.

ABOUT THE AUTHOR

Stella Bixby is a native Coloradan who loves to snowboard, pluck at the guitar, and play board games with her family. She was once a volunteer firefighter and a park ranger, but now spends most of her time making up stories and trying to figure out what to cook for dinner.

Connect with Stella on Facebook, Twitter, and Instagram @StellaBixby.

Stella loves to hear from her readers!
www.stellabixby.com

ALSO BY STELLA BIXBY

Novels:

Rylie Cooper Series

Catfished: Book 1

Suckered: Book 2

Throttled: Book 3

Tampered: Book 4

Whacked: Book 5

Bungled: Book 6

Snowed: Book 7

Wasted: Book 8

Magical Mane Mystery Series

Downward Death: Book 1

Bowling Blunder: Book 2

Spotlight Scandal: Book 3

Tango Trouble: Book 4

Spelunking Speculations: Book 5

Festival Fiasco: Book 6

Printed in Great Britain
by Amazon

31202993R00128